EVIL EVER LIVES

The ABC Files by Paul Masson

eBooks

Hamish Cameron Investigates

A Chorus of Evil

Evil Through the Spyglass

Evil Ever Lives

Evil in Summerland

Memories of Evil

In Paperback

The ABC Files: A Collection of Three Novels

Evil Ever Lives

Evil in Summerland

Memories of Evil

Evil Ever Lives

Paul Masson

Paul Robert Masson

ISBN 978-1-7382730-2-7
Publisher Paul Robert Masson, PO Box 1866, Niagara-on-the-Lake, ON L0S 1J0, Canada

First Printing in this format, 2024

Contents

Acknowledgements

I am grateful to members of the Niagara-on-the-Lake Writ-ers' Circle for helpful comments on parts of my manuscript, and especially to Eileen Campbell and Barb Babij. Many thanks also to Ann Watson, who extended my knowledge of Canada's justice system, though she is not responsible for the liberties I took in describing it. My wife Betsy provided encouragement and careful editing.

Ashcroft-by-the-Sea is an imaginary town, and any resem-blance of the characters in the *The ABC Files* to persons living or dead is unintentional.

Preface

Ashcroft-by-the-Sea, on the South Shore of Nova Scotia's Atlantic coast, was founded in the late 18th century by United Empire Loyalists. It retains many of the handsome brick and stone houses built in its heyday, though the sources of its early prosperity, fishing and lumber industries, have long since moved out or shut down. Now it's a retirement community-- occasionally called ABC--chosen by wealthy retirees from as far away as Toronto as the place to spend their golden years in pleasant surroundings and to breathe a bracing sea air.

Hamish Cameron was one of those, having retired at 75 as judge on Nova Scotia's Court of Appeals. However, circumstances led him to start a new career as a detective. He and Sean Carroll investigate some of the goings-on in their not always idyllic community. This is the account of the latest case of Cameron and Carroll, Investigators.

Map

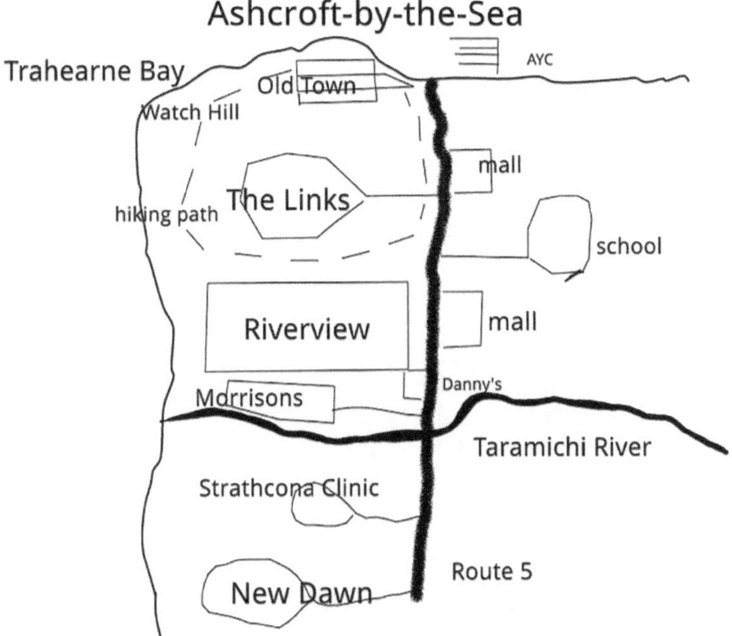

Map of Ashcroft-by-the-Sea
Evil Ever Lives

1

June 23, 2019

Quickly pulling on a pair of jeans and a sweatshirt, Sean Carroll combed his hair and stepped into a pair of running shoes. Grabbing his keys, he ran outside and jumped into his ageing Subaru to drive the kilometre to Olivia Lopes' house on Harrow Place.

A few minutes before, his pleasant dream of sailing with friends on a halcyon ocean had been interrupted by a strident ringing noise. As he emerged from sleep he fumbled for his cellphone.

Sean heard a high-pitched, panicked voice: "Sean? This is Olivia. Can you pick me up at my house? I need to leave! Now!"

"Olivia, why? What's the matter?"

"I can't talk. Just come as soon as you can! I'll be waiting outside." The call had ended abruptly.

Harrow Place was a quiet street of mansions built on large lots with spacious front lawns shaded by mature trees. Number

17 was dark, as were the neighbouring houses, and there was no traffic on the road. A little light filtered out from the street lamps, but not enough for Sean to pick out details in the front yard. He parked on the far side of the street, and cautiously got out of his car. The air felt damp, and there was dew on the ground.

As best as Sean could see, there was no activity either inside or outside the house, but he started up the long driveway toward the building to investigate. He checked the time on his phone: 4:15 am. Trying to be as unobtrusive as possible, as he approached the house he whispered, "Olivia. Are you there?" There was no answer.

He skirted around a dumpster parked in front of a garage door, evidence of the renovation work underway. It cast eerie shadows on the driveway. Sean crept along a brick path to the left that led to the front door. As he approached the house, he flinched as a spotlight mounted under the eaves came on, triggered by his movement. The light blinded him, and he put up his hand to shield his eyes from the glare. Looking around, his gaze fastened on an object near the front door. Lying beside the steps leading up to the entrance was something that looked like a body.

Sean thought back to last week's high school reunion. He had not seen Olivia for almost 30 years, but their meeting had revived the ache in his loins that he had felt for her throughout his time at Riverview High. Sure, she was older now, more mature, but he could still see in her the whimsical, charming, intelligent girl that she had been at eighteen.

2

Thirtieth Reunion, June 15, 2019

Early in June, business had been slow at Cameron and Carroll, Investigators, Ashcroft-by-the-Sea's one and only detective agency. Hamish Cameron, who was a retired judge with decided opinions, pontificated that everyone was too busy at the end of spring to hire a detective. "They are either winding up the school year, getting married, or making plans to go on summer holidays." Hamish was tall and thin, with a stern chin, a well-proportioned nose, and a high forehead, his distinguished appearance giving weight to his words.

Sean Carroll sat down at the board table in the office after shooing off the chair the resident long-haired black cat with yellow eyes named Stanfield. The detective agency was housed in his family's home–his, now that his mother had passed away. Sean was in his late 40s, with a pleasant round face and a thick head of brown hair. He was fit from jogging and sailing though he weighed a few more pounds than he would like.

As usual, he disagreed with his senior partner on principle: "No, I think it's the effect of spring on everyone's psyche. Just look at all the flowers and trees in bloom. We're all so happy that we don't make mischief for others."

For whatever reason, Sean had some free time so he decided to indulge himself a bit and attend the reunion of his 1989 class at Riverview High School. In the early years after his graduation he had been only too glad to get away from the school. Moreover, he had moved outside the province by the time of the first of the five-year reunions. Though back living in Ashcroft for the last half a dozen years, he had never felt the urge to participate in a get-together with his former classmates. The thirtieth anniversary seemed sort of special, however, and Sean decided that it was worth making a little effort to link up with some of those he had lost track of.

The weather was warm, and the perfume from the flowering lilac trees gave the evening a sultry, exotic quality that reminded Sean of his teenage years when he started becoming interested in girls. He drove to Danny's Bar and Grill, where the reunion was being held, across the street from the school. Danny was willing to close his place to regular business for a private party, all the more so because he himself had graduated from Riverview High thirty years before.

Sean arrived a little after the starting time of 8 pm. Over the entrance to Danny's, a modest one-story brick building, was draped a large banner with "Class of 1989" on it. Inside, the booths of the restaurant, upholstered in brown faux leather, were filling up. People were milling about the bar or getting name tags at the welcome desk. The dining room and the patio at the back were just large enough to accommodate the attendees.

As he entered, Sean saw a few vaguely familiar faces, though he couldn't put names to them. A full-figured woman with dyed blonde hair that did not match her brown eyebrows sat behind a table with a sign saying "Register Here." Sean wasn't sure that she had actually been in his class since he didn't remember her at all. She checked his name off a list and handed him a name tag, two drinks tokens, and a list of attendees. "Welcome, Sean Carroll. I remember you from chemistry class!"

Sean thought to himself that such embarrassing encounters were why he had avoided reunions until now. "Yes, I was the one who spilled sulphuric acid on himself, and the teacher had to get the school nurse to come and take care of me." He rolled up his left sleeve and showed her the scar on his wrist. Smiling apologetically, he peeked at her name tag, which only gave her first name, Jessica. Searching his memory he came up with a single classmate with that name, a mousy brunette who had been painfully thin. Taking a chance, he said: "Jessica Foster! How are you?"

She beamed. "I'm fine, though, it's Jessica Miele now, and has been for the past 25 years. I live in Bridgewater, and I have two kids who are through university and are living on their own!"

Sean nodded with the pretence of interest, thanked her for the update, and said he would wander around to meet his other classmates. First he went over to say hello to Danny, who was standing behind the bar. He was facing in the opposite direction taking drinks orders. Sean gave him a slap on the back: "How'ya doin'? Looks like a good turnout for the reunion."

Danny turned and smiled at him. He had dimpled cheeks and sported a jolly expression on his face that projected good cheer. He wore brown slacks and a pale blue, short-sleeved polo shirt. "Great to see you, Sean. We're expecting 120 people, including spouses, if everyone who RSVP'd shows up. You know, I've hosted this several times over the years, and it's interesting how much turnover there is. Some guys move away and don't come any more. Others, maybe like yourself, don't come at first but then they want to relive the past so they start to show up."

"You may be right. I've been thinking more and more about a girl I knew in school but haven't seen in decades, Olivia Lopes. She was glamorous and sophisticated, like a young Lauren Bacall starring in *To Have and Have Not*, but she only dated upperclassmen. I got as far as studying with her in maths class, but that was it. She was a goddess, someone who was way too good for me. What happened to her, anyway?"

"Well, she's supposed to show up here tonight, though without her husband, Larry Rizzo. Remember him? Not the sharpest knife in the drawer, but he could charm the fruit off the trees! Anyway, they married half a dozen years ago, but their relationship has had its ups and downs over the years."

"I thought they'd both moved away from town long ago."

Danny looked around to see if he needed to serve some more drinks, waved at someone, then continued. "You're right, but things are more complicated than that. Olivia enrolled at Eastern University, got bored, and came back to live with her parents for a year, when she took up again with Larry. I think you'd left town by then so you probably didn't hear about this."

"You're right, this is news to me. So then what happened?"

"They dated for a few months, while all her friends told Olivia that she was crazy to be wasting her time on this guy. So everyone was relieved when they broke up. But Larry took it badly, made some threats, and even roughed her up a bit. Olivia's dad called the police, who went out to talk to Rizzo's parents. You remember they lived beside the Taramichi River in a wreck of a house near the pulp and paper mill? Apparently the RCMP convinced them that Larry had better clear out of town if they wanted any peace and quiet, and that's what happened.``

"So how'd they end up getting married?"

"Hold on, I'm getting to that. Olivia spends a year living with her parents and decides to go back to EU. She gets her English degree and starts a career as an editorial assistant at a publishing house in Halifax. Larry Rizzo goes off to someplace that nobody knows anything about, except maybe his parents, and we all forget about him. But about twenty years later he comes back to town, comes into my bar and starts flashing money around. He drives a new Mercedes and says that he has an internet business."

"So he'd become a tech entrepreneur?"

"Apparently. Anyway, he ends up buying one of the run-down mansions in Old Town, but he lives in an upscale apartment building in Halifax, where he hooks up with Olivia again, who hasn't married but has become a successful, full-fledged editor. Apparently the old spark is still there, and after a whirlwind courtship they tie the knot."

"So she actually likes the guy? Or was she impressed by his money?"

"Who knows? Anyway, after they get married Olivia becomes obsessed with renovating the old mansion Larry bought and moves back to Ashcroft. They get a hot shot architect and the best contractor in the area to modernize the building and make it into a real palace. You've probably seen it, it isn't that far from your place. It isn't finished yet but Olivia lives there while continuing her work reading manuscripts for the publishing house. Larry apparently spends most of his time in Halifax at his apartment there."

"Danny, you're amazing! How d'ya know all this stuff?"

"Standing behind the bar, I hear a lotta things. Besides, Olivia comes in here from time to time."

After thanking Danny for all the background, Sean wandered around the room looking for familiar faces. He greeted a few guys with more enthusiasm than he really felt. He saw an old friend with whom he had long ago lost contact, and got a run-down of his life since graduation. The dream of becoming a writer had never panned out for him, and he sold real estate. They promised half-heartedly to keep in touch and Sean moved on.

Sean was starting to get bored when he spotted Olivia entering the restaurant. She was still stunning, and he had no trouble recognizing her, with her long brown hair, high cheekbones, and light olive complexion. She was wearing a stylish dark grey pant suit that complimented her still-slim body. Trying to appear nonchalant he edged over in her direction, attempting to get her attention before she got swept up by the crowd.

with them, sometimes coming back in the middle of the night." She added indignantly: "Something's going on there, and I have a right to know!"

Sean hesitated before replying: "I guess I can do that, but if you don't want your husband to know it's going to be tricky. I could check up on company filings, but I'm assuming that your husband's firm is not a public company so I'm not going to be able to look at his financial statements. The best I can do is ask around and stake out his office."

"Okay, do what you can. But don't under any circumstances reveal to him that I'm behind your inquiries. I hate to think what he'd do to me."

"Listen Olivia, it's not up to me to say it, but I think you want to consider contacting the police if your husband makes you fear him like that."

Olivia bit her lip, and looked down, but didn't answer.

"So how shall we communicate? I need you to tell me what you know about his company, people he works with, and so forth. Can you give me a cellphone number, or can we arrange to meet?

"I can tell you about the business right now. It's called UModel.ca and it's an internet platform for would-be models to post videos of themselves and get exposure to modelling agencies. The site has taken off recently, they get a lot of business and Larry says it's very profitable. They have a small office in Halifax. That's all I know."

"OK, it's a start. I'll do what I can."

"I live at 17 Harrow Place. I know where you live, you're nearby, and I have your phone number. When I'm free, I'll call you." She gave him a tight smile and walked back to the group on the patio, her weaving figure reviving sensuous memories in Sean's mind. He threaded his way through the crowd to his car in the parking lot. On his way home, Sean thought about his final year of high school.

3

Ashcroft-by-the-Sea, 1989

The town was bustling in those days, mainly because the Riverview subdivision had been recently established and houses were going up there at a rapid pace and selling like hotcakes. The Riverview primary, middle, and upper schools had just been built. Most of the old mansions in Ashcroft-by-the-Sea dating back to the boom years of the 19th century were still occupied. However, many were run down or divided up into apartments. A few were abandoned, waiting either for demolition or for a rich purchaser willing to sink money into a bottomless pit.

Riverview was growing quickly, and was taking on its own identity, with its shopping mall, a few office buildings, and of course its public schools. Indeed, Riverview was now outshining its namesake, Ashcroft-by-the-Sea, of which it was nominally a suburb. Families that had moved to the area mostly came because they had children of school age, and the school system had a good reputation. Many came from Halifax to escape the urban environment and to find a safe place with plenty of outdoor activities to raise their kids, even if it meant commuting back to the big city.

The school became a focal point. The heroes of the town were the football and hockey players, especially in those years when Riverview beat their rivals from the neighbouring towns. But other sports were also given prominence--basketball, track and field, lacrosse, even archery. The sporting events were not just for the students; the parents also attended in large numbers and quite a few crowded around station wagons or panel trucks to enjoy a tailgate party before a game. Moreover, the school buildings hosted public meetings, since aside from churches there were no halls able to seat a large number of people.

Sean thought back to his last year in high school, when he shared a number of classes with Olivia. He was good at maths, and Olivia was too, so they were both in the advanced placement calculus class. They compared notes after class, and helped each other do the homework. Olivia was the class president, a top student as well as a cheerleader. With high cheekbones, lustrous long brown hair, and with a perky sense of humour, she was attractive as only a girl who is becoming a woman can be. She displayed modest grace as well as a merry laugh. Though not assertive she had her opinions and was not afraid to voice them. Sean was fascinated by her.

All the boys her age wanted to date her, but until this year she had always gone out with older boys. One day Sean felt bold enough to ask her if she wanted to see a movie on the weekend.

She looked at him with a condescending smile and said "I don't think so." That was the last time he dared try to talk to her about anything but school subjects.

He thought back to when the school year was about to end, and those in grade 12 were excited about going to the prom but worried about not having a date. Sean had been seeing a girl off and on and was expected to ask her to go with him, but he would have invited Olivia if he thought there was a chance she would accept. She was presumed to be the queen of the prom, and the betting was that she would go with Anthony Thompson, who was also in grade 12. He seemed sophisticated and mature, and got reasonably good grades despite not studying very hard. He played tight end and captained the football team. He had caught a few touchdown passes and was a solid player, but would not get any football scholarship. Not that he minded, since in any case he was going to the college where his father had gone, and his family had plenty of money to pay for it. He never made much of an effort to excel, because he didn't need to. His family would look after him: help him find a job, get him into the right clubs, and give him money as an advance on his inheritance.

Sean remembered another boy in his class with a very different family background who was also seen with Olivia. Larry Rizzo was a dark horse. His family was poor, and he hadn't covered himself in academic or athletic glory, but he had charm and ambition. He was short in stature and thin, but had a puckish face and laughing eyes. He had been chatting up Olivia and she hadn't been completely oblivious to his charm. Sean heard from the grapevine that she had been seen walking hand-in-hand with Larry.

The Lopes were a respected local family. Olivia's father was Ashcroft's doctor. His office was located in a building next to the Fairweather Mall. He had bought one of the earliest and nicest houses in Riverview, a spacious centre-hall-plan in a large yard graced with mature trees, where Olivia lived.

The Rizzos, in contrast, lived in a run-down farmhouse that was located between Riverview and the Taramichi River, near to where Morrison's pulp and paper plant stood. The roof of the house leaked and the yard had the musty smell of wet wood when the wind blew from the direction of the plant. Larry's father did various odd jobs for people, and was said to supplement his meagre income by poaching and cigarette smuggling. Larry's mother helped feed her six children by mending other peoples' clothes and growing vegetables in a small garden next to the house.

Larry failed his grade five, but he used his charm to convince the Principal that he merited to go on to the next grade. In grade nine he and some of his buddies formed a band, and had some success in getting gigs at local events. In the next year he started to take serious interest in girls, and broke a few hearts as he worked his way through the field. But he didn't come near Olivia until grade 12, and that was outside of school since she was taking advanced courses to prepare for university while he was stuck in classes for the academically challenged. He started talking to her while walking to school, passing her bus stop near Route 5 along the way. He would greet her with a joke every morning as he went by, and after a month or so she started walking to school with him, which after all was almost across the street from her house.

They never even considered dating. Olivia by this time was between boyfriends, her beau, who was a year older than herself, having gone off to Mount Allison University after graduating from high school. Though she flirted with a few of her class-mates and went on dates, she had decided not to have a steady boyfriend this year but instead to wait until she had enrolled at university. She was not sure, in any case, which one she would attend, nor even whether she wanted to study arts or science. The future seemed wide open to her.

As the date of the prom approached Larry had to decide whether he wanted to go and whom to invite. The prom would cost money to rent a tuxedo and buy his date a corsage, but he had saved a little cash from playing in the band so he could afford it. Never shy when it came to the opposite sex, he decided to invite Olivia. *What the hell, the worst she can do is turn me down!* So he introduced the idea to her as a joke on one of their walks to school. "Olivia, if you showed up at the prom with me, the whole town would be in an uproar! Wouldn't that be fun?"

She laughed. "It might be worth it just to see people's faces! But I'm not saying yes or no yet."

If she did go with Larry, it would be an amazing déclassement for Olivia.

But Olivia was not concerned about being conventional but instead liked to chart her own course. The idea of being accom-panied by Larry germinated within her. She let him know that she would not reject an invitation from him out of hand, but did not promise to accept it either.

The alternative for her would be to go with Anthony Thompson, though he hadn't asked her yet. But they were almost certain to be queen and king of the prom, and it was a tradition, though not an obligation, to attend the prom together. Olivia was everyone's choice as queen because of her academic achievements, charm, and position as class president, and Anthony because of his success in sports and general popularity. Moreover, he was attractive, elegant, and rich. They would make a fine couple arriving at the prom in the red Ford Thunderbird convertible that he was given by his parents when he turned 18.

Larry made the mistake of dropping a hint to one of his buddies that he might be escorting the prom queen to the event, and the rumour quickly spread and reached Anthony Thompson. He was furious. "How can that no-good nobody dare pretend that he is going to take her! I'm going to cut him down to size!" He rounded up a couple of his football friends after school and cornered Larry in the parking lot behind the gym. "You keep away from Olivia Lopes, you no-account! We'll give you a preview of what you'll get if you don't." He and the two others hit him in the stomach, bloodied his face, and, as he lay on the ground, Anthony kicked him a few times in the groin.

Olivia had expected an invitation from Larry, but when she didn't get one she accepted Anthony's. Larry had not shown up at school for a week. When she asked one of his siblings what had happened to him, she was told that he wasn't feeling well. When she saw him again he was walking with a limp and did not say much to her.

The prom was not the triumph that Anthony had no doubt expected it to be. The day before the big event his Thunderbird was stolen. It was later found wrecked in a ravine that led down to the Taramichi River. The police blamed a joy rider but never found the perpetrator. Anthony swore revenge if he ever caught the person who did it.

4

The Body

Sean carefully approached the mansion at 17 Harrow Place to investigate what he had seen by the steps. He followed the brick path from the driveway to the front door to avoid leaving any footprints on the dew-covered grass. When he got to the foot of the steps that led up to the entrance, he could see that the body lying there was that of a man. The tragic expression on Sean's face changed to relief. *At least it's not Olivia.*

The body was clad in a tan raincoat that was open, revealing a pair of brown slacks and a short-sleeved tee shirt that was stained with blood. Around his neck was a gold necklace. The man was spread-eagled on his back and appeared to be dead, but Sean did not attempt to touch him to verify it. He leant over to look at his face. Though he had not seen him for thirty years, he recognized Larry Rizzo. He took out his cellphone and took a photo. Next he called the number that Olivia had used to contact him. The call went to voicemail, and Sean left a message for her to call him. He then called Joe Washington, another schoolmate of his who now commanded the RCMP detachment located in Lunenburg, which provided policing for Ashcroft. Joe had been one of the few black students in his class. He was the star running back of the Riverview football team. After university, which he had attended on a football scholarship, he joined the RCMP and diligently worked himself up the ranks.

Joe arrived about twenty minutes later in a cruiser, its roof light flashing, driven by a uniformed constable. Still fit looking, Joe had a muscular frame and measured just over 6 feet. The two of them came over to Sean, who was standing in the drive-way. With a stern expression on his face, Joe said: "I hope you haven't touched anything? Sean, I'm going to ask you to stay in your car until we've examined the grounds, and then we will want a statement. Is there anyone in the house, do you know? How did you happen to be on the scene?"

Sean hesitated, then said: "I got a call from the woman who lives here, saying she was in some danger and wanted me to pick her up. She didn't explain, but it sounded urgent. When I got here, she'd gone. That's all I know."

Joe Washington's cursory look at the body revealed a bullet wound in the chest. Stepping carefully, he rang the doorbell but got no answer. He and the constable cordoned off the front yard, and Joe called headquarters to arrange for a medical examiner to be sent to inspect the body. While the constable took photo-graphs of the scene, Washington approached the car where Sean was sitting in the driver's seat with the window wound down. Washington looked at him suspiciously. "So, what's the name of the woman who called you? How is it that she called you in particular in the middle of the night--do you know her well? And do you have any idea who the dead man is?"

"The woman who lives here is Olivia Lopes, and I think the body is that of her husband, Larry Rizzo. You must remember him? As for Olivia, I hadn't seen her for thirty years until last week's class reunion, where she asked me to do some detective work."

Joe looked sceptical. "And she called you In the middle of the night? And what did she want you to investigate?"

Sean shook his head: "I can't tell you what she wanted me to investigate, it's confidential information between me and my client."

Washington bridled. "You're not a lawyer, you have no right to refuse to answer questions in order to protect your client. I'm starting to wonder whether you're not more involved in this crime than you claim. I'm going to ask you again what task you've been given, and I would advise you to answer my question fully and truthfully."

"She asked me to investigate a personal matter, that's all."

"And why would she call you in the middle of the night to come over here? Did she know her husband had been shot?"

"She didn't tell me."

"We need to find her, since as of now she's a suspect in a homicide investigation. It appears that she's not in the house. Give me any contact information you have for her."

"OK, here is the number that she called me from." He took out his cell phone and showed him the call log.

Washington growled at him: "I'm going to need more information than that, and if you refuse to cooperate, then you and

Hamish can forget about renewing your Private Investigator business licence. When we get through examining the crime scene I'm going to need a formal statement. Come to the detachment office tomorrow afternoon. And I don't want you to interfere with our investigation in any way, or do any detective work on any aspect of this case. If Olivia Lopes calls you again, tell her to contact my office."

Thus dismissed, Sean drove back to his house, The Oaks, his family's homestead, a big ramshackle mansion in need of some repair which he shared with Hamish Cameron, and which also served as the office for their detective agency. It was beginning to get light just as Sean got back into bed, exhausted by what had happened.

When he awoke, the events of the previous night gnawed at him. *I have to find Olivia*, he thought to himself. *She may be in danger.* He tried the number stored on his cellphone, but again didn't get through to her. *I hope the police are actively looking for her.* He turned on his laptop and got on the UModel.ca website. Despite Joe Washington's order not to interfere, he had to find out more information about Rizzo's activities.

The website explained that would-be models could post their videos for free, but potential employers would pay a commission in order to be put in contact with them. The videos were made with varying degrees of professionalism. Some showed a young woman sashaying across the floor, wearing a long dress that seemed to be home made, and others just jeans and a t-shirt. Still others had elegant couturier outfits, or posed in swimsuits, smiling at the camera. Some poses were suggestive, if not outright provocative, the model swishing her dress to reveal her lack of underwear or showing a naked breast. There were also a few male models in the videos. None of the men or women was identified by more than a first name and the name of a city or region.

Sean learned that potential employers first had to become charter members and pay a monthly fee before they were allowed to contact a model. The website explained that those applying for charter membership were vetted to make sure that they were legitimate modelling agencies, fashion designers, or advertisers. UModel would make arrangements for them to interview a particular model for a fixed charge, and would serve as intermediary in the negotiation of a modelling contract, charging 25% of the contract fee as commission.

The "About Us" tab on the home page listed Larry Rizzo as the head of UModel.ca, and Andrew Leipzig its general manager. Rizzo's bio said that he was a Silicon Valley entrepreneur, while Leipzig's, that he had extensive experience in Los Angeles' fashion industry. The location of other UModel offices was not specified, but Sean found that there were both UModel.ca and UModel.com websites, each with a different list of models and contact information.

Further research on the internet revealed that Andrew Leipzig had worked at a fashion model agency in LA, but did not uncover other details. Sean tried again to contact Olivia, without success. Then he received a call from Joe Washington, asking him to come to the detachment office to give a statement.

*****

Sean showed up at Lilydale Road half an hour later, going to the reception desk and saying that he had been asked to come in by Washington. The young woman at the desk asked him to sit down to wait. After 15 minutes, he went back to the desk and asked whether Washington still wanted to see him, and was told it wouldn't be long. Five minutes later, a constable came up to him and invited Sean to accompany him to the interview room. He was led to a windowless room containing a table with a hard-back chair on either side of it. The constable motioned him to take a seat, then left the room. Sean waited another 10 minutes before Joe Washington came in.

"Hi Sean. We've made some progress on this case but we need answers from you now. You're the person who found the body and are the person who is mixed up with the wife of the victim. So we need your story before we go any further."

"Am I a suspect?"

"At this stage of the investigation, anyone who knew him is a potential suspect. And we are still looking for his wife, Olivia Lopes. Have you heard from her?"

"No, nothing. And I resent being treated as a suspect. After all, I called in to report the discovery of a body."

"Well, it wouldn't be the first time a perpetrator tried to deflect suspicion by contacting the police. And it's clear that you know things that you don't want to share with us. That, and the fact you're romantically involved with the victim's wife makes you a person of interest."

"What do you mean, romantically involved? She's just a client."

"That's not what I hear. You've been an admirer of Olivia ever since both of us were at Riverview High School. It was well known then, and it's evident now by the way you're trying to shield her from questions."

"Listen, either you charge me or I'm leaving. I came here to give a statement, but I know no more than what I already told you."

"OK, OK, Sean, you've made your point. I've typed up the story you told me last night, and I want you to read it and confirm that you know nothing about the circumstances of last night's events other than what's in there."

Sean read through the statement and signed it. "So now am I free to go?"

"Sure. But I don't know why you are playing it this way. What do you hope to gain? You should be helping the RCMP find Olivia, she may be in danger. Where do you think she's gone? I repeat that if you hear from her you have to get her to come and tell us what she knows about her husband's murder."

"I'll tell her if I do. But I've no idea why she wasn't at the house when I arrived, nor where she's gone. She doesn't answer her phone."

Sean left the RCMP detachment, and decided to stop on his way home at Olivia's parents' house in Riverview, which he remembered from his school days. Olivia's father, Dr. Alexandre Lopes, a short, dark-haired man in his 60s, answered the door, and looked questioningly at Sean.

Sean explained that he was looking for Olivia, and hoped they could help him locate her. He added that he was concerned for her safety, given that her husband had been found dead in front of their house in Old Town.

Dr. Lopes was at first struck dumb by Sean's words. Then he said: "Oh my god! Who did this? I always thought Olivia's marriage to Larry Rizzo was a mistake!"

Sean tried to calm him, saying that there was no evidence that she had been hurt. "Where might she go to hide? If you hear from her, tell her to contact the RCMP. They can protect her if she's in any danger."

"She's staying with us. The renovation of their house in Old Town is going through a busy phase, so she decided to stay here for a few days. Come on in, you can talk to her."

As Sean entered the hallway, Olivia appeared behind her father, a cup of coffee in her hand. She wailed, "Did I hear right? Larry has been killed?"

When he nodded, she collapsed to the floor. Sean and Alexandre Lopes lifted her gently to her feet, and she regained consciousness. They walked her back to the kitchen, and sat her down at the breakfast table. Her father made a fresh pot of coffee and poured out three cups. Sean had mopped up what he could of the coffee using paper towels.

Olivia was shivering in her short-sleeved blouse and Capri pants, despite the mild temperature outdoors. "Larry and I had an argument about why he refused to tell me about his business. I said that I would have to find out about it myself then, and he exploded. He said I would regret it, and stormed out of my bedroom. I got dressed in a hurry and decided to move back to my parents' house for a while. I've been here since yesterday evening."

Sean looked curiously at her. "So why did you call me at four in the morning?"

"But I didn't! What do you mean?"

Sean wondered if the shock of hearing about Larry's death had given her selective amnesia, so he did not insist. He added: "The police are actively looking to talk to you. You need to contact Joe Washington at the RCMP's Lunenburg detachment as soon as possible."

"How did my husband die? Do they have a suspect?"

"I don't know. He was lying near the front door when I got there. According to the RCMP, he was shot. But they are just starting their investigation. As one of the last people to see him alive, you are likely to be the police's prime suspect in the absence of other evidence."

Olivia reached out and laid her hand on Sean's arm. "You've got to help me! I don't think I can face the police now. I'd like some time to get myself together."

Sean patted her hand but shook his head. "That's not possible. You've got to contact the RCMP right away and make a statement. Talk to your lawyer first, and follow whatever he advises. I'll try to provide what help I can, don't hesitate to call me."

Her father reached out to Olivia, putting his hand on her on the arm. "We'll look after you. But you must get in touch with Joe Washington. They need to know where you are."

Olivia nodded her head. "OK, I'll do that. But Sean, please don't tell the police that I've asked you to investigate my husband. It wouldn't look good."

Olivia got out her cell phone to call her lawyer, and Sean left the kitchen so that she could talk privately. When he returned a few minutes later, she said that it was all set, the lawyer would pick her up in an hour and accompany her to Lunenburg so that she could make a statement. He would call Joe Washington to notify him in the meantime of Olivia's whereabouts.

"That's good, Olivia. It's best for you to get that over with. Do you have any idea who might have wanted to kill Larry? You might be in danger too."

She frowned. "I don't think so. It must be due to his business dealings. I'm sure the police will come to that conclusion."

"Now, can you tell me more about UModel.ca? Where are their offices located? And who did Larry have working for him?"

"It's a very small operation in Halifax, on Connaught Avenue. The only person I know there is Andy Leipzig, but there's also a woman who handles the office work. Andy seems to be knowledgeable about the fashion scene, what models would appeal to the agencies, and so forth."

"So did Leipzig negotiate with the agencies when they expressed interest in a particular girl? And what was Larry's involvement with the day-to-day operation of the business? I thought his role was in setting up the company, not running it."

"Larry wouldn't answer my questions. That's why I wanted you to look into what's going on there."

When the lawyer arrived Sean accompanied her outside, he had a lump in his throat as he waved goodbye. Sean got into his ten-year-old Subaru and drove home.

5

UModel

Sean was in the kitchen at The Oaks when Hamish returned from Halifax where he had been visiting his long-time lady friend, Izzie French. Hamish was tall and distinguished looking, as befitted a former judge, now retired. He usually displayed a stern expression, but it was belied by his twinkling eyes. Sean filled him in on what had happened.

Sean wanted his opinion on whether he should go ahead with the investigation or heed Joe Washington's warning to cease and desist. "If he finds out that I've disobeyed him and carries out his threat, it might put Cameron and Carroll at risk."

Hamish thought for a moment and said: "He really would need a court order to prevent you from doing your job. After all, you took a commission in good faith. I would just make sure that you don't run afoul of the RCMP's investigation."

"My idea is to probe how UModel works. If Olivia's right, Rizzo's murder may be the work of some of the shady characters who seem to be associated with the business. I really need to talk to someone who has put up their modelling photos on the website. But I don't know how I can get access to their contact info."

*****

Kimberly Weedon followed the instructions of the photographer, looking into the camera and smiling, walking along the Bay of Fundy, and staring off into the distance. He was a neighbour of her best friend Sophie, and had agreed to take a few fashion photos of them. They had met him at Avonport Beach. The day was windy, but there was enough sun for him to take some stunning photos.

Kimberly and Sophie were only 16, but they had heard about this website called UModel where they could put up photos and videos of themselves. Who knows, they might even get a modelling job! It would be a hoot in any case. Sophie was the more mature of the two, and her parents liked her to be independent. She wasn't going to tell them about UModel, but she wasn't too worried if they found out. Kimberly, on the other hand, knew there would be hell to pay if her parents found out. She asked Sophie, "Are you sure this is not going to get back to them?"

Sophie shook her head. "All you have to do is not give your real name, and make sure your parents don't answer your phone or read your email!

Kimberly was a tall girl with a nice figure, on the thin side, who could pass for 20. With her flowing blonde hair and pale skin, she was the epitome of a northern beauty, like her mother who was of Finnish descent. She was enthusiastic about the photo shoot, as if she had been waiting impatiently for this moment all her life. She asked the cameraman in an excited voice: "Should I wear some of my jewelry?"

The cameraman discouraged her: "No, it's best for you to have a natural look. It goes better with your colouring."

When they were done, Kimberly got onto the UModel website with her laptop and registered under a made-up last name and false address. The form contained a privacy notice that assured the user that information would not be shared without the permission of the person providing it. She would be listed on the website as "Kimberly from Nova Scotia."

"Well, that should do it," she told Sophie. "I've given my cell number and email in the contact information. I'm so excited! This was fun, and I'm looking forward to learning about the modelling business!"

*****

When Sean got back to Ashcroft at the end of the afternoon he found Olivia sitting in the detective agency office, which was installed in a former dining room of The Oaks. The room was furnished with some of its original furniture, plus a few filing cabinets and a desk. Olivia sat at the dining table, which now served as a board table. She had come to tell him about her interview by Joe Washington at the Lunenburg detachment office.

"He asked a lot of questions about my marriage. I didn't tell him about the argument with Larry, just that we were not spending much time together lately because of his job and the house renovation. He wanted to know about Larry's business, and I gave him the same info I gave you."

"Did he ask you why you had hired me, and what you wanted me to look into?"

"Yes, and I told him I just wanted you to look into some of Larry's business associates. I think he bought the explanation, because he didn't pursue the issue further."

'Good. So I guess he doesn't object to my continuing to work on it -- assuming you still want me to?"

Olivia sniffled: "Yes, I'm convinced that one of them must have killed Larry. I can't believe he's gone! We had our ups and downs, but he was the love of my life ever since high school. He was charming, witty, and could make me laugh! Though he had his faults, he was a good man at heart."

"Did Washington give you an idea of who he thinks shot your husband?"

"No, but they've dusted the house for fingerprints and are trying to figure out who was there last night. Or it's possible, given the position of the body, that he came outside when some-one rang the doorbell, and was shot then."

"Are you sure you didn't call me? By the way, I've rung the number that woke me up at 4 am and all I get is voicemail."

"Let me see the record of your calls." When she looked at his phone, she said definitively: "That's not my cell number. Some-one else must have called you."

"But I was sure it was your voice! How can this be?"

Olivia looked perplexed: "It all doesn't make sense to me." She sighed.

Sean looked over at Olivia with concern. "Let me take you to dinner tonight. You need to unwind, start to put this tragedy behind you and get on with your life. Let's go to Danny's, have a steak or something."

Olivia hesitated, then said, "OK, sure. Let's do that. Just let me stop at my parents' place so I can change my clothes."

6

Danny's Again

Sean waved to Danny when he and Olivia walked into the dining area. It was furnished with Formica tables and chairs upholstered in dark brown faux leather. With the low ceiling the effect was both retro and yet somehow warm and comfortable. They sat at a booth and waited while Danny came over. He greeted them warmly and gave them each a menu. While Olivia was glancing down at hers, Danny looked at Sean and raised his eyebrows. Sean looked away, his face reddening at the implication that he was dating a very recent widow.

"Good to see you both," Danny said, "The special is a beef brisket with green beans and mashed potatoes. Can I get you something to drink?"

They settled on a beer for Sean and a margarita for Olivia. She was dressed soberly but elegantly in a grey pants suit, and her stop at her parents' home had allowed her to renew her make-up. She looks ravishing, Sean thought to himself.

"Let me fill you in on what I've found about Larry's business. It looks to be on the level, but to make sure I'm going to try to contact some of the models who have posted on the UModel website. We'll see what happens next. What do you intend to do about the business?"

"I'm having my lawyer look into how it's set up. It's a partnership agreement, and he needs to find out the terms under which the other partner or partners can buy out Larry's share. I certainly don't plan to keep any ownership in UModel."

"How did Larry happen to get involved with the fashion industry? What did he do after he left Ashcroft? Did he go to California?"

"Larry always kept his cards close to his chest, even with me. But he told me when I first saw him in Halifax, after he had settled there, that he had gotten involved in financing start-ups in the LA area."

"Well, he must have made some serious cash somehow to be able to provide financing, if it was his own money. He didn't start out rich. Maybe he was serving as a middleman."

"That's probably the explanation. He certainly knew people with money. I overheard part of a conversation he had with one of those guys who showed up at odd hours, who said that his boss could see his way to keeping Larry on retainer for ten grand a month. I never got a good look at him, and I don't know his full name, Gus something. He'd just flown up from New York City. His boss apparently has a summer home here in Nova Scotia."

"I'll see if I can track him down. You need to know what sort of activities Larry was involved with in order to decide what to do with his assets. I assume he left a will?"

"Yes, we both made wills last year. What he owned comes to me, after small legacies to his five brothers and sisters. His parents have passed away. Nothing is specifically mentioned. So I don't know what's in the estate, aside from the apartment in Halifax and the house at Harrow Place, and their contents. If you're willing to look into it, I'll tell my lawyer that you will help him track down Larry's assets and liabilities. Just coordinate with him, would you?"

"Sure, I can do that."

They finished their drinks just as the waitress brought them their entrees, the beef brisket. As they dug into the food, Olivia said, "Let's not talk about all this anymore. Tell me about yourself, Sean. What have you been up to for the past 30 years, and how did you make it back to Ashcroft?"

"After graduation I went away to university out of province. After my science degree, I got a job in computers, moved to Toronto, and got married. My wife and I drifted apart, and, when I got transferred to Chicago, we split up. I had a good job, but in tech, it helps to be young and freshly trained, and I decided to take a generous buy-out a few years back."

"And you came back here?"

"My mother died, and after debating with myself for a while I decided to return to live in The Oaks. I did some volunteering, got involved with Hamish Cameron in investigating the retirement residence where he lived, and we went on from there to start a detective business. As they say, 'the rest is history'!" Sean laughed.

"Sounds like an interesting life. Mine's been pretty boring. I like my editing job but it could hardly be described as exciting!

I guess that's why I fell for the glamour that Larry represented when he returned to Nova Scotia. We'd been friends in high school, and when I saw Larry again I still thought that he was the one for me. Despite my parents' objections, I married him six months later. I've been wondering for some time whether it was a mistake. As they also say, 'decide in haste, repent at leisure'!"

Sean sipped a glass of red wine. He was starting to feel mellow, and this added to the pleasure of being with Olivia and having a real conversation with her for the first time in his life. His contented smile gave place to a frown when he noticed that Anthony Thompson had just entered the bar. Olivia had also noticed him, and was trying to hide her presence by turning toward the wall and pretending to look through her purse.

The ruse did not work, however, and Anthony came striding over and stopped at their table. Ignoring Sean, as he had at the reunion, he addressed Olivia: "Hi Livy! How are you bearing up? Can we get together tomorrow as planned? We can catch a meal on the waterfront in Lunenburg and go from there!"

Olivia's face turned scarlet, and she said, "I'll call you." Turning to Sean, she said: "We've got to go now," and she grabbed her purse, preparing to get up.

Anthony looked scornfully at Sean, then said to her, "Don't forget! I'll pick you up at your parents' place at 5."

Sean hastily paid the bill and drove her home. They did not say much to each other along the way.

7

The Modelling Office

Sean drove to the address given to him by Olivia for the Halifax bricks-and-mortar location of the online modelling agency. He parked on the street in front of a nondescript six story office building. The premises of UModel were on the third floor, and Sean looked for suite 310 when he got off the elevator. A narrow glass door, flanked by a glass panel on either side, had "Modelling Services" painted on it. Sean opened the door and walked into a small waiting room with three armchairs placed on a Persian carpet. Photographs of female models adorned the walls. A reception counter was installed in the far wall from the entrance door. Behind it, Sean could see a young woman busily typing away at a computer keyboard in an office with filing cabinets and business directories placed on a bookcase next to her desk. She wore a pair of glasses with black plastic frames that matched the colour of her dark shoulder-length hair.

"What can I do for you?" she asked pleasantly.

"I have an appointment with Andy Leipzig. I phoned you earlier. You must be Jane."

"Yes. Mr. Carroll, is that right? I'm sorry to say that Mr. Leipzig was called away, and he didn't know when he would be able to get back."

"Perhaps you can help me. I'm representing Mrs. Olivia Rizzo and assisting the lawyer who is settling her husband's estate. Can you provide me with financial information concerning UModel, and tell me how the company was set up?"

"I'm afraid I can't do that without Mr. Leipzig's permission."

"Then please pass on my request to him." Sean said, not hiding his annoyance. He gave her his card. "Tell me, what do you do in this office? Isn't UModel a virtual modelling agency – is there a need for a bricks-and-mortar operation?"

She hesitated, then replied "When a client identifies a potential model from the information online, he can arrange a meeting here where the terms of a contract are hammered out. We prepare the paperwork and keep track of contract fulfilment."

"Do you also keep files on each of the models?"

"Only if she signs a contract with one of our clients. I say 'she' because most of our models are female, but a few of them are male."

"Very well. Please pass on my request to Mr. Leipzig. And I would like you to schedule another appointment with him."

"I'll call you after I speak to him."

*****

Having returned to the detective agency's office, Sean decided to look into Anthony Thompson's activities while he waited to hear back from UModel. The reunion committee had circulated short bios of the attendees. Thompson's address was listed as a townhouse in Old Town, and his professional activity was described as working as an investment banker. Sean hadn't realized that he now lived so close to him. *Anthony's place must be about halfway between 17 Harrow Place and The Oaks. I wonder if he and Larry crossed paths at all. I'll have to ask Olivia.*

Sean knew that Anthony's parents still occupied the Thompson family homestead, a large estate situated out Route 5 past the Taramichi River. As Sean recalled, it included a hobby farm that bred horses. No doubt Anthony would one day inherit it, since he was an only child. A quick check online of the employer Anthony had listed revealed that he worked at the family's financial firm. *I'll bet his main qualification for the job was having the Thompson last name. He didn't have to work hard to get that position!*

Sean stopped by the *Ashcroft Examiner* office to chat with his friend Terence McGovern, the editor. He was about Sean's age, and had a beard flecked with grey. "Terry, what do you know about Anthony Thompson? He must have made the society pages over the years?"

"He certainly has. He's been considered Ashcroft's most eligible bachelor for decades now. If you look through back issues, you'll see that he and his family have hosted a fair number of galas and fetes, and he has often had his picture taken as a chairman of some charity supporting a worthy cause. He also has been written up for his success on the polo field."

"No scandals or arrests for drunk driving or the like?"

"No, not that I can recall. He's lived in a gilded cage, everything taken care of for him, a conventional and proper existence, though he does have a weakness for young women. These days he is often seen arm-in-arm with women half his age."

Sean hesitated, then asked: "I hear he was romantically involved with Olivia Lopes once, when she was still single."

Terry looked at him quizzically. "Yes, I had heard that too, but it probably wouldn't be in the paper. What's your interest?"

"Just idle curiosity. I saw them at the reunion speaking together as if they were old friends."

Terry shrugged his shoulders. "Any idea of where the investigation of Larry Rizzo's death might lead? We did a story on your finding the body, of course, but just reported the bare facts. The RCMP has been very quiet about the case."

"Joe Washington has pointedly told me not to stick my nose in it, and he hasn't given me any indication of who his suspects might be. The trail is likely to lead to Larry's business associates, if you ask me." He wrinkled his brow: "By the way, do you know anyone from New York City with a summer home nearby? Or an employee of his named Gus? Apparently they had some dealings with Larry Rizzo."

"Well, there's that big house down the coast, the old Wildman mansion. It's been bought by a rich American, though I don't know his name. You could look it up on the real estate website."

8

The RCMP

When he got home he looked up the property Terry had mentioned on Nova Scotia's Property Online website. Cameron and Carroll had a paid subscription, so he could access it directly. The listing gave a certain Jerry Farthing, resident of New York City, as the owner of the property since the previous year. An internet search of that name turned up an investment banker who lived on East 62nd Street in Manhattan. *This might well be the person who's bought the Wildman estate*, Sean thought.

His research was interrupted by a phone call. "Sean? This is Joe Washington. Would you come into the detachment office? Our investigation has turned up some new information, but also more questions about your role."

"I told you all I know, which is very little. I haven't seen Larry Rizzo alive for years. What more can I tell you?"

Washington's tone had none of the warmth that character-ized their dealings in the past. "Just come in, or we'll come out to The Oaks in a police vehicle with flashing lights."

"Okay, I can be there in about half an hour."

*****

On his way over Sean thought to himself what evidence could possibly involve him. He had not once met Larry Rizzo since they had been at high school together. Most of the time since school one or both of them had been outside Nova Scotia, and they had never crossed paths. His contact with Olivia was recent, and only related to the commission she had given Cameron and Carroll to investigate her husband's business dealings. *I wonder if the RCMP wants to rake me over the coals for continuing my investigation for her. But I can rightly claim to be doing so at the request of the executor of Rizzo's estate.*

Once again Sean was shown into the interrogation room, this time without a wait. There were three chairs this time, and Sean was soon joined by Joe Washington and a man who intro-duced himself as Superintendent Robert Klijs. "I am in charge of the Rizzo investigation," he added pompously. Klijs was heavy set, wore thick glasses, and appeared to be about 40. He turned to Washington and nodded for him to begin.

Joe seemed nervous, as if there was some tension between the two police officers. "Sean, you have the right to remain silent and not answer our questions. Moreover, you have the right to retain and instruct counsel."

"Am I being detained or accused of a crime?"

Joe continued, "No, but you may be at some time in the future. Our investigation found your fingerprints on a soft drink can in the dumpster in Rizzo's driveway. Can you explain how it got there?"

Sean stared at him. "No, I cannot. I certainly didn't put it there."

"You did not have anything to drink with you when you found the body on June 23rd?"

"No, I did not."

"Had you visited the house before the night of the murder?"

"No, never."

Washington shook his head with annoyance, then continued. "Let me turn to another matter. You say you received a phone call from Olivia Rizzo around 4 am and immediately got dressed and drove to the house owned by her husband, arriving at roughly 4:15 am. You called me at 4:30 am, and reported finding a body. My constable and I arrived at 4:50 am, and saw you standing in the driveway of the Rizzo home. Is that correct?"

"Yes, that's right."

"The medical examiner's report says that Larry Rizzo died of a gunshot wound around 4 am, so by your own admission you were on the scene about the time of his death."

Sean showed his frustration. "So what? He sure was dead when I got there!"

Washington continued: "Another thing. The early part of your story doesn't jibe with testimony given by Olivia Rizzo. She claims not to have called you. Is it possible that you imagined it? Maybe it was part of a dream?"

Sean shook his head in bewilderment. "I'm sure it was a real call, and it was her voice. I showed you the number in my call log. But she says it didn't come from her cell phone, it was from another number."

Joe frowned sceptically, and continued: "Furthermore, she was at her parents' house all evening, which is confirmed by her father, and hence would not have asked you to rescue her from 17 Harrow Place. That would explain why she wasn't there when you showed up."

"Well, someone called me. I wasn't too awake, but the voice would have to be a pretty good impersonation to make me think that it was Olivia."

Klijs inserted himself into the questioning: "Are you sure you don't want to change your story? It just doesn't add up. You don't really expect us to believe that you're just an innocent bystander in this whole thing?"

"But it's the absolute truth!" Sean shot back indignantly.

Klijs snarled: "In that case, we're going to prepare a written statement based on your responses to these questions and ask you to sign it. Lying to the police is a criminal offence and if we find proof that's what you've been doing then you are in big trouble. I should also warn you that you are now a person of interest to the police in the death of Larry Rizzo and may be charged with his murder, or with abetting it. You are hereby warned not to try to leave the province."

9

Hamish Weighs In

When Sean arrived back at The Oaks, Stanfield was lying on the only comfortable chair in the office. The cat looked up pityingly at him, yawned, and went off to nap somewhere else. Stanfield seemed to sense that Sean was not having a great day.

He told Hamish the gist of his interview with Washington and Klijs.

Hamish was flabbergasted. "You shouldn't have gone there without a lawyer! You know the saying, 'A person who acts as his own lawyer has a fool for a client.' It's not that you should hide the truth, it's just that you don't know the whole picture so some of your answers to the police questions may come back to bite you. Now they are on the record, you're going to have a hard time reeling them back."

Sean looked abashed, and shook his head: "I don't understand how they can claim that I didn't get a call then, since I have a record of it on my phone. They should be looking for the phone that made the call."

"I'll bet they looked for it, but couldn't identify the owner. And there's nothing to say that it was a call for help from Olivia, as you maintain. Let me give you some advice: I'd consult a lawyer before you volunteer any more information. You seem to be the main candidate for his murderer, since you are the only one known to be on the scene around the time he was killed. And the fact that Olivia denies making the call puts you at odds with your client. I suggest you refuse to do any more work for her."

"I don't think that's right. She's had a rough time, and needs all the help she can get."

Hamish looked at him sternly. "This is a murder investigation, not a class reunion! You seem to be trying to relive your high school days, when you fell in love with Olivia Lopes. You've got to look after your own interests. You can't let yourself get entangled in something you know nothing about. For all you know, she might well have shot her husband. "

Sean looked uncomfortable: "I can't believe that. Olivia would never do such a thing. Anyway, she has an alibi. She was with her parents."

"I think you're letting your feelings get in the way of your judgement. Another thing: what progress have you made in identifying Rizzo's business associates or talking to any of their models?"

"I'm working on it."

"Well, I would make that a priority."

*****

The old Wildman mansion was much as Sean remembered it, at least from the outside. A long driveway wound its way up to the house on a treed lot, its lawn immaculately maintained. He parked in a layby beside the three-car garage. Sean noticed a late-model Audi TT coupe in the garage, which was open. He rang the bell, hoping for a domestic who might be garrulous about his or her master.

An elderly man opened the door, walking with a slight stoop. He was dressed formally, with a dark suit but no tie, his dress shirt unbuttoned at the top. With his long face and grey hair, he had a slightly lugubrious air. "Yes, what can I do for you?" he said in a firm voice.

Thinking that he was a butler, Sean said, "I would like to speak to Mr. Farthing, please."

The man gave a little smile. "That's me. And you are?"

Sean quickly switched gears. He took out a card, and handed it to Farthing. "I'm Sean Carroll, of Cameron and Carroll, Investigators. We've been hired by an insurance company to track down a hit-and-run driver. The victim was only able to read part of the car's licence plate." Sean recited a subset of the characters on the tag that he had seen on the back of the Audi in the garage. "Did you or someone else drive your car into Halifax three days ago and get involved in an accident?"

Farthing shook his head. "That's not possible. I had this car transported from the States in a car carrier last week, and only yesterday did I get Nova Scotia plates put on it. It's hardly been driven here."

"OK, that seems straightforward enough. Do you mind if I look at the car to see if there are any dents on the hood?"

"No, go right ahead. If there are any, I'll want to get back to the moving company in any case."

Sean made a show of walking around the car, noting that the rest of the garage was empty of vehicles. The Audi seemed brand new, with no dents or evidence of body work done. "Yes, I can see that this isn't the car that was in a collision. Thanks for your time." As he turned to go, he added; "You've recently moved here?"

"Well, I'm only planning to stay part of the summer. This is a vacation home."

Sean raised his eyebrows, and grinned. "Not a small cottage!"

The man laughed. "I like to entertain."

Sean looked around appreciatively at the expansive grounds and the flower beds flanking the front door where rhododendron bushes were blooming. He could see a large patio in back, leading to a fence that surrounded a pool. "You could certainly have some great parties here!"

Farthing shrugged his shoulders, and turned to go back into the house.

Sean excused himself for taking up the man's time, got in his car, and drove home.

*****

When he got back Hamish was in the office looking at a letter with a frown on his face. "Look at this," he said, handing Sean a sheet of paper.

The page had words cut out of a newspaper glued to it. It read: "Hamish Cameron, you are going to pay for your sins. Romans 6:23."

Sean asked, "What's this all about?"

"I don't know. I just looked up the reference, which is 'For the wages of sin is death ...' but I have no idea which alleged sin of mine this refers to."

"It sounds as though you are being threatened. Be careful when you go outside. I would call the police as well, though I don't know how receptive they will be."

"Maybe it's just a practical joke. The way I see it, the wages of virtue are also death. That's just our lot as mortals."

"You're not very concerned about something that could be a death threat! I wouldn't shrug it off lightly. I'm sure you made some enemies while serving as a judge."

"You know my philosophy. 'Life is a bad joke, but it's better to laugh at it than cry over it.'" He chuckled. "In any case, I'm going to wait and see if I get another letter before I call the RCMP. But in the meantime I'll contact Sam O'Leary of the Halifax Regional Police to see if anyone I sentenced in my time on the bench has just been released from prison. I can't think that anything I've done since my retirement would provoke this type of letter."

10

Modelling Opportunities

Kimberly Weedon got an email from the UModel agency, inviting her to come into the Halifax office for an interview. She was excited. *This is my big chance! But if I tell my parents, they'll forbid me to go.*

Getting to Halifax would be a problem for her since she didn't have her driver's licence yet. But when she told Sophie the news, her friend said that she was planning on driving there to go shopping. She would be happy to go on the day of Kimberly's appointment and give her a lift.

The next day they drove into Halifax right after summer school. Kimberly had told her mother that she was staying after class but would be back for dinner. She and Sophie managed to get away after lunch because they just had sports in the afternoon.

Along the way to Halifax they swapped stories about boy-friends and clothes. Sophie teased Kimberly: "I saw you smiling at Jim. So is he your new bae?"

Kimberly reddened a little, but put on a scornful face. "No, he's too immature. Not my type. And what about you? Are you getting serious with your boyfriend, now that your parents are away?"

Sophie laughed, but instead of replying, said: "I'm going to the Halifax Shopping Centre to look for clothes, they have all the best stores. It's awesome! Where do you want me to drop you?"

Kimberly said in an excited voice, "The modelling interview is on Connaught Avenue, not far from the shopping centre. My appointment's at 3, and I expect I'll be done by 4. I'll text you."

Sophie dropped her off, and she took the elevator up to the third floor and entered the door at 310, labelled Modelling Ser-vices. The receptionist rose from behind her desk and unlocked the inner door, inviting her into an interview room that was next to the office where she worked. "If you would just wait here for a few minutes, the gentlemen will be here shortly." Kimberly passed on her offer of bottled water.

The room had a couch with a coffee table in front of it and two armchairs, with wall-to-wall carpeting. Kimberly sat on the couch. There was a window that looked out over the street, but without much of a view. She picked up a copy of *Chatelaine* magazine and leafed through it.

After five minutes two men came in. The younger one introduced himself as Andy Leipzig, saying he was the head of UModel. He then introduced the other man: "Jerry Farthing knows a lot of influential executives in the States who are looking for talent. He could launch you on a career as a top model."

Farthing smiled at her, looking her over. "You could be just the fresh new face they are searching for. Have you done any photo shoots already? The ones on the internet don't do you justice. I can arrange to have a portfolio of pictures taken of you at my place. I'm hosting a group of ad executives next Saturday who are looking for a face to launch a new campaign. Can you attend?"

Kimberly laughed nervously, excited by the prospect of making it into the modelling business so quickly. *This is my big chance! But how can I get away from home? My parents will never allow it.* She answered hesitantly: "I'll try to make it, but I'm not sure."

"We can send a car for you. Just give us the address."

Kimberly thought for a few seconds. *I'll figure out something. I'll give them the name of the nearest supermarket.* She said to Farthing: "You could pick me up outside the Sobeys in Windsor."

"Fine. I'll send Gus, my chauffeur, to pick you up there at 8 pm."

They said goodbye, and Kimberly took the elevator down to the street, where she texted Sophie: "Can U come now?" As she waited, she strolled up and down the sidewalk, looking at the churches nearby.

Sophie was excited when she arrived in front of the building 15 minutes later. "How did it go? Did you get a job?"

"No, but I'm going to a party on Saturday at the house of someone who's big in the fashion business. He's going to get me to do a photo shoot and then I'll be interviewed for a modelling job by ad executives who are going to be there!"

"That's awesome!"

On the way home, she and Sophie arranged a story to tell her parents. Kimberly would ask their permission to attend a sleepover at Sophie's Saturday night. The party and photo shoot at Farthing's house would probably mean getting back to Windsor in the early hours of the morning. She would ask to be dropped off at Sophie's, spend the rest of the night there, and return home later on Sunday. Sophie's parents were away, so she had the place to herself.

Sophie was excited for Kimberly. "Wow, what an adventure! But is it really safe to go alone? I could come with you," she said tentatively.

"Well, they didn't say anything about that. Anyway, they must be Okay, UModel's a professional outfit. They're even sending me a car! What should I wear?"

"Why don't you look at my wardrobe? We're the same size, let's see what looks good on you. I'll lend you the clothes for your big night," she said enviously.

When she got home, Kimberly didn't say anything about her afternoon to her parents, who assumed that she had gone to lacrosse practice as she often did in the afternoon.

11

Old Grudges

Hamish received another anonymous letter the next day, again with a message pieced together from cut newsprint, which he recognized as the font used by the *Chronicle Herald*. This letter said: "All who sin apart from the law will also perish apart from the law. Romans 2:12." Though Hamish was not particularly concerned, he called Sam O'Leary of the Halifax Regional Police. "Sam, I'm getting anonymous letters and I wonder if they are coming from someone whom I sentenced in court. Could the timing reflect the fact that a convict has just been released from jail? I'd be grateful if you could find out if any of the people on a list I've put together have recently got out. I've identified a few who might be in line for release, but I don't know what their parole status might be."

O'Leary was someone Hamish knew from his time on the bench, since the police officer had frequently provided evidence to the court. "Sure, Judge, I can do that. I'll check the names on your list and let you know."

*****

Sean had not heard from Olivia since their dinner at Danny's. He wondered if she had met Anthony in Lunenburg as planned. The nature of their relationship gnawed at him. He kicked himself for being jealous, but he couldn't escape the obsession he had for her and his resentment of Anthony. He decided to give her a call.

She did not mention her activities since their dinner, but said: "I've been invited to a party given by an associate of Larry's on Saturday night. Want to come along? It might be a chance to find out more about the activities of UModel. I met the host, Jerry Farthing, once, but don't know him at all. I just know that he hires models for ad agencies, serves as a sort of middleman, perhaps working with UModel in some capacity. I still haven't heard back from my lawyer about the details of UModel, how it's set up, nor whether my husband and Jerry were actually business partners. Hopefully he'll help us sort things out."

"Funny to hear you mention his name. I went to his house last week to look him over, making up a story that I was trying to locate a car that was involved in an accident. He knows I'm a private detective. Do you really think I should come?"

"Why not? He can hardly throw you out."

"Once he sees me, he's going to be suspicious and won't reveal anything to you. You might ask Anthony to accompany you, if you don't want to go alone." Sean couldn't hide the resentment in his voice.

Olivia was silent for a few seconds. "I guess I owe you an explanation. Anthony and I used to be close friends, but that was a long time ago. There's nothing between us now. I'd rather go alone to the party than invite him to accompany me."

Sean's jealousy was partially allayed by her explanation, though he wasn't sure that he completely believed what she'd said. "OK, then why don't you go alone, but you can call me if you change your mind."

*****

O'Leary rang Hamish back. "There's a couple of inmates on your list who were recently released, within the last six months that is. First is Ravi Singh. Remember him? I investigated his case. He was a small-time drug dealer, but he got into a fight with another one and was convicted of manslaughter. He claimed that it wasn't his doing, the other guy had attacked him and he was just defending himself. You sentenced him to 15 years, and he was let out after 10."

"Yes, I remember him. He broke down after the sentence, saying that his family depended on him and would be reduced to begging."

"The second one I found was a burglar named Clement Benedict who had three previous convictions and was sentenced in lower court to 10 years in prison after being caught red-handed coming out of a house that he had just robbed. When you were on the Court of Appeal you turned down his lawyer's request to have his sentence reduced."

"Thanks Sam. I'll see if I can track them down if you can give me the addresses that they provided when they were released."

12

The Party

Kimberly couldn't wait for Sophie to pick her up. She had packed her pyjamas and clothes to wear tomorrow in an overnight bag, as if she were going for a sleepover. Sophie came by at seven and they drove back to her house so that Kimberly could get dressed for the party.

Sophie fussed over her, combing her hair and helping her with her makeup. Sophie lent Kimberly a long dress that she had bought for herself on their trip to Halifax. "You look so hot! Are you sure I can't come with you? I don't think you should go to the house of someone you don't know just because he dangles a modelling career in front of you."

"Sophie, you know they didn't say I could bring someone. I'll tell you all about it when I get back. I'll have them drop me here. I should have had them pick me up here too, but we hadn't agreed on the sleepover idea then. Anyway, I'm ready now and it's almost eight so we'd better head over to Sobeys."

Sophie waited in her car while Kimberly stood in front of the entrance to the supermarket. A Lincoln Town Car, which they hadn't seen because it was parked behind some other cars, slowly pulled up. The driver was dressed in a grey uniform, and a cap was lying beside him on the seat. He said: "Are you Kimberly? Then hop in, I'll take you to the party. My name is Gus." Kimberly got in the back and waved to Sophie as they drove off.

They headed south and it was almost an hour before they got to Jerry Farthing's house. Kimberly tried to get some information about her host, but the driver was not very talkative, so eventually she just looked out the window. When they turned into the drive leading up to the Wildman mansion she marvelled at the size of the house. The layby near the garage was full and there were cars parked on the grass along the driveway that led from the road to the house.

Gus took the loop in the driveway that led up to the front door and got out to open the door for her. As she entered the house, the doorman offered to take the light jacket that she had put over her party dress, and she went through to a large space that must have once served as a ballroom. It was crowded with people who were standing and talking loudly, ignoring her. Feeling lost, she sighed with relief when, from an adjoining room, Jerry Farthing came out and took her arm. "I don't know anyone here!" she said.

"Well, then let me introduce you." Still holding on to her arm, he approached a group of men wearing tuxedos and women dressed in long flowing dresses. "This is Kimberly. She is going to be a famous model one day!"

One of the men gave her a grin, which she thought seemed a little sardonic. She did not say anything, just smiled and nodded. *So this is the world that models inhabit. These people are a lot more elegant than those I know in Windsor!* She goggled at their fine clothes, the jewelry of the women, and the house's luxurious decor. The room was ringed by tables displaying oriental vases and bookcases containing leather-bound volumes.

As a waiter carrying a tray of champagne glasses went by, Jerry motioned to him and took two glasses off his tray. He offered one to Kimberly, saying "You're old enough to drink, aren't you? If not, we'll just pretend you are."

Kimberly took a sip. *So this is champagne. It tastes like pop with vodka in it.* She said to her host: "It's good. I think I could get used to this!" She drained the glass.

"Don't worry, there's plenty more of it!" He beckoned the waiter over again, and took another glass for her. He guided her around the room and introduced her to several other groups of guests, then said: "After you finish your glass, let's do the photo shoot."

He took Kimberly through a doorway and down a hall to the back of the house. Unlocking a door at the end, he motioned her to go into a sort of den, with a large tan leather couch and several matching armchairs. Sliding glass doors led outside to a patio. An imposing-looking tripod was sitting in the middle of the floor. "We'll do it here. I'll get the cameraman. Just make yourself comfortable in the meantime."

While she waited, she looked around the room. A shelf at one end showcased picture books. Most of the covers displayed beautiful women. She picked up one of them, entitled *Italian*

Beauties, and noticed that the pictures showed the models wearing few or no clothes.

She plumped down on the couch. Her head was starting to spin from the effects of the champagne. Jerry came into the room, accompanied by a man with a large camera held with a strap around his neck. "This is Roger. We'll take a variety of shots with different poses, to show you off to the ad agency executives."

Roger put his camera on the tripod, and motioned to her to lie back trailing one leg on the couch, the other on the floor. Then he took several photos of her profile, and others of her looking up to the camera from the couch. After a quarter of an hour of photos, Roger said that he had enough and would print them and put them into a portfolio. Jerry ushered him out and locked the door.

He sat down on the couch next to her. "Now we can take some more intimate photos. You don't mind, do you? I won't show them to anyone else. It's just that you have such a beautiful body." He put his hand on her thigh, and stroked it.

Kimberly tried to stand up but she found that the champagne made it difficult to do so. She protested: "I don't want to!"

Jerry put on a pained expression. "But you want me to get you modelling jobs, don't you?" He left implicit the bargain he was proposing.

"This is not what I agreed to! I want to go home!" She made a greater effort this time and rose unsteadily to her feet.

Jerry took a placating tone. "Of course, I won't force you to do something that you don't want to do. Just sit down for a moment and we can discuss the next steps in your modelling career."

*****

Olivia remembered the Wildman mansion from her youth. Not that she had ever been inside, but she had occasionally driven by it. The Wildmans were an old Boston family, and generally only stayed in Nova Scotia during the summer months. Cyril Wildman had died several years before, and his heirs had finally found a buyer for the place. Houses of that size and price were not easy to sell.

She was curious to meet Jerry Farthing again in order to learn what she could about his dealings with UModel and her late husband. She drove up toward the house and managed to squeeze her car into a space on the lawn beside the driveway, which was parked up for almost its full length. She got out and, after smoothing her black dress, walked up to the front door.

She nodded to the doorman and looked around for her host. She turned back and said: "I don't see Mr. Farthing. Is he around?"

"Not at the moment, Madam. I think he has some business to take care of."

So Olivia wandered around the room, nodding to people she didn't know. She picked up a glass of champagne, and looked at the pictures on the wall, but they didn't tell her anything about the host of the party. Indeed, she wondered if they had been bought just to furnish the house.

She turned back toward the other guests, and espied someone she did know who had just arrived -- Anthony Thompson. He seemed to be unaccompanied, and had not joined any of the groups of other guests. He was dressed casually in a dark coloured turtleneck and slim fitting black slacks. He came over and said hello.

"What a surprise! I had no idea that you would be here," she said guardedly.

Anthony responded with a smile. "Nor I, that you would be invited."

"Do you know our host well?"

"Not really, just through business dealings."

"Oh, what does that involve?"

"We are both in the financing business, but some of my clients need to raise US funds, and need a contact in New York. I can do the same for some of Farthing's American clients with interests here in Canada. And you, how did you cross paths with him?"

"Apparently he and my husband did business together, but I'm not sure what. Do you think that Farthing helped finance UModel?"

Anthony shrugged his shoulders, and said: "It's possible." He did not seem to want to elaborate. Their conversation turned to the other guests. Olivia and Anthony were speculating about whether they had flown up from New York for the party when Jerry Farthing emerged from a doorway at the back of the room. He first walked over to someone standing near the entrance and talked quietly with him. Then he looked around the room and approached a few guests who had recently arrived in order to welcome them.

After a few minutes he made his way to where Olivia and Anthony were standing. "Greetings to both of you, I'm glad you made it. Olivia, I was so sorry to hear what happened to your husband. Sorry and shocked! Do the police have any leads?"

Olivia shook her head. "Not that I'm aware of, sadly. Tell me, what business did you have with my husband? Do you have a continuing interest in UModel?

Farthing shook his head vaguely. "No, I sometimes do favours for my clients that extend beyond financing. For instance, if an ad agency needs a new face, I direct them to UModel. Larry Rizzo and I crossed paths long ago in LA, and we kept in touch over the years. But I didn't have any direct dealings recently with him. As for UModel, I assume that it will just keep going under Andy Leipzig's lead. He is supposed to be here tonight, by the way, but I haven't seen him yet."

Anthony shook his head. "No, he's not around. But I understand you have something for me?"

Jerry took his arm and guided him out of earshot, so Olivia went over to two young couples who were talking in loud voices, curious to learn where they came from. She introduced herself as a local and was told that they had flown up from White Plains in a private plane owned by one of them. "Are you good friends with Jerry?" Olivia asked.

"We live fairly close to one another and we're members of the same country club as Jerry. This is our first visit to Nova Scotia for all four of us! We're staying here at the house but have rented a car. We fly back on Monday. Tomorrow we hope to do some sightseeing."

Olivia gave them some suggestions of things to see in Halifax, the South Shore and the Bay of Fundy, each of them more than enough to occupy a day. While they were chatting Olivia looked over to where Jerry and Anthony were talking. She saw Anthony nod, and follow the other man to the doorway at the back.

Olivia wished her new-found friends a pleasant Sunday of sightseeing, and strolled toward the place she had last seen the two men. As she was about to enter the doorway, a man stepped in front of her, and said politely, "I'm afraid that's off-limits to guests."

"Oh, sorry! And who are you?"

"I'm Gus. I work for Mr. Farthing."

Olivia backed away, and joined another group of guests. She chatted casually with them, discovering that they were from Halifax. "So how do you know Jerry?"

One of the men responded that Jerry was on the board of a theatre there, and that is how they had met.

Olivia commented: "I had no idea he had connections in Halifax."

The man gave a small laugh. "Yes, he's known for his interest in young actresses." He raised his eyebrows. He added, "I gather that his house purchase here is designed to get him closer to the action."

Olivia's phone rang. She excused herself and stepped away. "Hello?"

"Olivia, it's Sean. I just got a call from a girl called Kimberly Weedon, who is my nephew's daughter. She's at the party, a tall blonde who is still in her teens. She was invited by Jerry Farthing, but he's harassing her. She wants to get away from him. Can you drive her home?"

"I haven't seen anyone like her at all."

"Apparently she was lured there in order to do a photo shoot and meet some ad executives about a new product launch, but now Farthing wants to take some nude photographs of her."

"OK, I'm on it."

Olivia marched back to the doorway leading to the back of the house. When Gus blocked her way again, she said to him: "I'm going to get that teenage girl that your employer lured here. If you stop me, you'll be guilty of an indictable offence." She continued down the hall past him. He let her go, but took out his cell phone and rang a number.

She didn't see anyone at first along the hallway. A kitchen branched off to the right, but no one was there. In a room to the left there was a bar where a man wearing a white jacket was pouring the contents of a bottle of champagne into a number of fluted glasses sitting on a silver tray on the counter. He glanced up briefly then turned back to his task. Olivia kept going. She heard some voices but could not locate their source. She tried a door to her right, but it was locked, so she knocked. A voice which she recognized as Jerry's said: "Just a second, I'll open it."

When the door opened, she looked into a sparse storeroom that contained various food supplies and beverage bottles on shelves around the room. He had a bottle of champagne in each hand. Jerry smiled at her. "What's the matter? Is there anything I can do?"

Surprised not to see anyone else there, she blurted out: "What have you done with the teenaged girl that you lured here?"

Jerry's face had a puzzled expression. "What girl? I don't know what you mean."

"Her name is Kimberly Weedon. Now where is she? I'm going to take her home. If you don't produce her, I'm going to call the police."

"I have no idea what you're talking about."

"Then show me what's in the other rooms back here."

"I'll be happy to." Jerry put down the bottles and led her out of the storeroom. Heading further along the hall, he opened the doors of other utility rooms. At the end of the hall, he used a key to unlock the door of a room that appeared to be a lounge and that contained a large camera tripod in the middle. The room was empty, but Olivia observed that there was evidence of recent occupancy, namely three half empty champagne glasses on a coffee table in front of a sofa. "So, who was here then?"

"I wanted to show Anthony a book from my library."

"And the third glass?'

Jerry swallowed before replying with an ingratiating smile; "You don't expect me to reveal all of his secrets, do you?"

Olivia stormed out, and returned to the reception room, noticing that Gus was no longer at his post. She looked out a front window and saw a limousine winding its way down the driveway onto the highway. She called Sean. "I didn't find her, but I'm guessing that Jerry's chauffeur is taking her back home. I'll stick around a little longer just in case she's still here. Call me if you hear from her."

She looked for Anthony but he did not reappear. Andy Leipzig came through the front door and waved to her but did not stop to talk. Instead, he went through the hallway door, apparently looking for Jerry Farthing. He reappeared a few minutes later with Jerry. The two were talking animatedly in low voices, but when Jerry saw Olivia staring at them he touched Andy's arm, and they stopped talking. Jerry walked over to where Olivia was standing, followed by Andy. "You know Andy Leipzig, I believe? He was an associate of your late husband's." Then he left the two of them together.

Andy put on a concerned smile. "What happened to your husband must be devastating to you. If there's anything I can do to help …"

"Actually, there is. What is the ownership structure of UModel? Is it a partnership? If so, what are the arrangements for disposing of a partner's interest?"

"Our Halifax operation and UModel.ca are owned by a partnership between your husband and me, but UModel.com is actually incorporated in the US with offices in several US cities. We're an offshoot of that company, but independent from it. Our partnership agreement specifies that if either partner becomes incapable of devoting the time and energy to the business, then the other partner takes over complete ownership, with no compensation owed to the leaving partner."

"So his death would mean that his estate would have no claim on the partnership's assets?"

"That is correct."

"And was my husband a shareholder in the US company?"

"Not to my knowledge. But you should check with them directly. Tell your lawyer to get in touch with me and I will give him the necessary contact information, as well as a copy of the partnership agreement."

"What was my husband's role in the 'Halifax operation,' as you call it?"

Andy paused, then said: "We follow up with the requests from potential employers to interview models, and help negotiate contracts between them. That's why we need to have a footprint in Canada, because employment regulations are different here from those in the US. And we need to be familiar with the types of local ad campaigns. What appeals to people in one country or region is not necessarily the same as in another country or region, and that matters for the type of model that ad agencies want to hire. We chose Halifax because Larry knew the territory."

"So what was he actually doing?"

"As I said, he acted as a middleman between employers and models."

"And why did people show up in the middle of the night and get Larry to go off with them?"

"Well, you know, sometimes there are late night photo shoots, and, say, the model turns out not to be quite right for the part so we have to find a replacement. That sort of thing." He did not appear to want to elaborate.

"OK, I'll get my lawyer to contact your lawyer, and they can sort this out. Are you planning to keep the Halifax office open?"

Andy appeared vague. "We'll see. It hasn't been decided yet."

13

Kimberly

The Town Car was speeding along the route they had taken earlier in the opposite direction. Kimberly wiped away her tears, then gritted her teeth. *They shouldn't have treated me that way! What do they think I am, anyway?*

After Jerry had started stroking her thigh, and she had asked to go home, he had promised not to have her do anything she didn't want to do. He explained that he had an important ad company executive at the party, who wanted to talk to her and look at her photos. He told her to wait there, he would get him to come to meet her and to have a look at the portfolio that the cameraman would have put together by now. The three of them would sit down and discuss her suitability for the job.

Kimberly played along with this story but she was still mad and no longer trusted Jerry. When he left the room Kimberly pulled out her phone and rang her father's uncle Sean. She thought he was the best person to call, because she knew he worked as a detective. She didn't want to have to explain where she was to her parents, and Sophie wouldn't be able to help.

She didn't have time to explain all the details but Sean was understanding and alarmed for her safety. He promised to try to arrange for someone he knew at the party to give her a ride back. "Don't worry, we'll get you out of there. If needs be, I'll drive down there myself."

Jerry came back with a tall man dressed in a turtleneck and slacks. Somehow he seemed more elegant than the other men dressed more formally in tuxedos whom she had met at the party. He smiled at her and explained that the ad agency had been hired to launch a new line of cosmetics to appeal to a younger demographic. She seemed like the perfect girl for the job. But to offer her a contract he would have to see her naked in order to be sure that she was the right girl. After all, this was a big opportunity and if she got the job, she wouldn't regret it later.

At that point Kimberly felt her anger boil over. She stood up and yelled that she wanted to go home. Jerry and the tall man looked very annoyed, as if they expected her to understand the simple logic of what they were saying. She wondered if they would let her go, so she looked for a way to escape. The glass doors leading to the patio were close to where she was sitting. She thought that if she could dash outside, she could evade them for long enough to get around to the front of the house. They wouldn't dare touch her in full view of the other guests.

A phone rang, and Jerry reached into his pocket to answer it. All of a sudden his anger changed to concern. He turned to Kimberly: "OK, OK, we'll take you home. Anthony, would you take her outside to the Town Car, and I'll get Gus to join you there. I'm going to look after my other guests. He then turned to Kimberly and said sternly: "Not a word of this to anyone. We'll deny everything and you'll have lost any chance to become a model." He hurried out to the hall while the other man gestured for her to come with him outside.

Kimberly, though still suspicious, followed Anthony through the patio doors to the car, which was parked behind the house. Gus joined them a minute later and they drove down the driveway to the road.

From the car, Kimberly looked carefully at the route they were taking to make sure they were going back to Windsor. When they reached the outskirts, she directed Gus to Sophie's house. He stopped in front but didn't bother to get out and open the car door for her, which was fine. She pushed it open, slamming it after bolting out, and ran up the stairs to the house. Fortunately Sophie was still up, and she opened the front door right away. Kimberly burst into tears and threw herself into her arms.

After telling Sophie what had happened Kimberly rang Sean again. "I'm safely back at my friend's house. I didn't think they would let me go but something happened to make them want to get rid of me."

"It may be due to the person I mentioned, Olivia, looking for you. Anyway, you get a good rest. I want to talk to you in the morning though. Can I stop by Sophie's house, say at 10 am or so?"

Kimberly agreed, and suddenly she felt very tired. She crashed in the spare bedroom, and was asleep in minutes.

*****

The next morning Sophie let Kimberly sleep in, so when Sean and Olivia showed up at 10 she was still in bed. Sophie took them up to her bedroom, and the three of them sat down in various spots around where Kimberly was lying to talk about the night before.

Sean chastised Kimberly for making a foolhardy attempt at getting into modelling. "This shows a complete lack of judgement which could have had serious or even fatal consequences for you. I'm going to have to tell your parents about this, and they're not going to be happy that you lied to them about what you were doing this weekend."

Kimberly bowed her head, dreading the punishment she would get from her parents. "I know I did wrong. But I thought it was going to be my big chance, and if I didn't take it I wouldn't get another one!" She snuffled into a tissue.

Olivia chimed in: "We seem to have flushed them out. I wonder if my husband was involved with this."

"With what?" Sophie asked.

Olivia said bluntly: "Procuring girls for sex with the promise of a modelling job."

Sean nodded. "It's obvious that the modelling offer from Jerry Farthing was completely bogus, that they are only trying to lure girls into displaying themselves, and perhaps more."

Olivia frowned. "Well, what do we do now? We can't go to the police, since Kimberly went willingly to the party, and they didn't force her to stay. We need to find out more about this first."

Sophie said hesitantly, "I suppose I could pretend to be interested in modelling and see if they invited me."

Kimberly laughed bitterly. "Get real. I know that you wanted to come too, but this would be going too far! I don't think you'd enjoy what I went through."

Sophie stuck out her chin. "But I would know what was involved in advance, unlike you. If we don't stop these guys then nobody will! And I think I can defend myself if I have to. I've been taking judo lessons."

Sean rubbed his chin thoughtfully. "It's too dangerous. I wouldn't want to take responsibility for this. Your parents would never allow it."

"They've always wanted me to be self-reliant. They're adventurous types, into sky-diving and trekking in the high mountains. If you can set up an escape route for me, I think they'd be on board."

Sean said: "No, it's too risky. It's not worth your being the bait in a sting operation."

They left Kimberly to get dressed, then Sean and Olivia took her back home. Sean explained to her parents what had happened. Kimberly had disobeyed her parents and lied to them.

Her mother turned to her angrily. "How could you do this, Kim? Do you know how foolish you've been? This almost led to a tragedy!"

To make sure that she would remember this lesson when she was tempted to do so again, they grounded her indefinitely: no after-school activities, no parties, and no visits to friends' houses until they decided that she could be trusted.

14

The Accident

Back at The Oaks, Hamish told Sean that he was becoming more concerned about the threats contained in the anonymous letters, since he had received another one. This one said: "Depart from me, you cursed, into the eternal fire prepared for the devil and his angels. Matthew 25:41."

Sean told him: "You need to contact the RCMP about this. Do you have any suspects?"

"Sam O'Leary gave me the names of two recently released convicts who appeared before me or whose appeal I rejected. One of them is named Singh and seems less likely to quote the Bible, but you never know. The other, Clement Benedict, sounds like two popes' names. He should be up on biblical references." He laughed.

"You'd better suggest to Joe Washington that they look into what he's been doing since he left prison."

But when Hamish called him Joe said he was too busy, there was nothing to go on, and quoting bible verses wasn't a crime. Besides, Sean Carroll was a person of interest in the murder of Larry Rizzo so the force didn't want to be seen as doing the detective firm any favours. Hamish slammed down the phone.

"That son-of-a-bitch is still bitter that we showed up the RCMP last year when they couldn't locate the missing girl who had been abducted, Kristy Oliveira, and we solved the case for them."

"That's right, and he also resents your contacting the Justice Minister's office directly in the case of New Dawn, when we identified the scams they were pulling on the residents of the retirement home. It was our testimony that got Guy Laframboise and Art Gibson convicted of medical malpractice, and Jerry Adams of fraud."

Hamish controlled his fury with difficulty. "If they're not going to do their job then I'm going to contact Benedict's parole officer to get his address, then try to find out more about the guy."

"Be careful. He might actually mean to kill you."

Benedict's parole officer gave Hamish his address without problem. Hamish was well known among the law enforcement community. They didn't much care if he was still a judge or not. In any case, he was on the side of law and order.

"What's he like?" Hamish asked the parole officer. "Is he the type to cite bible verses?"

"Apparently he got religion while in jail. This was his fourth stretch, and the longest one. Besides, he's getting old now, he's almost 60. So maybe he's worrying about the hereafter." He coughed. "Sorry about the reference to age, Judge."

"No offence taken. So is Benedict likely to be capable of murder? Does he hold a grudge to that extent?"

"I doubt it, unless he's a very good actor. He seems to have reformed while in prison and seen the error of his ways. I would say that he doesn't think he was wronged. Instead, he realizes that he did wrong. But we'll see if he keeps that attitude now that he's out."

Thanking the parole officer, Hamish decided to drive to the neighbourhood where Benedict lived and look around. He packed an overnight bag and warned Sean not to expect him back before tomorrow, since he was planning to spend the night with Izzie. He threw his bag into the trunk of his Prius, which was parked in the driveway facing out, and headed off.

He turned onto the street that led down to Route 5. The next corner had a four-way stop, and he noticed a car starting to cross the intersection from the right. He put his foot on the brakes, but nothing happened. Panicking, he reached for the handbrake but not in time to prevent his car from plowing into the other car, which was already in the middle of the intersection. Hamish's Prius stopped abruptly, and the airbag inflated, pinning him to his seat. The impact caused him to black out.

Sean heard the crash. Looking out the window, he saw that the Prius impaled on the other car in the intersection. He ran out to find Hamish wedged behind the wheel by the inflated airbag, apparently unconscious. Sean used his mobile to call 911, then cautiously opened the driver's side door.

The airbag was deflating, and Hamish's eyelids finally fluttered. In a quavering voice he said: "I braked at the intersection, but the brakes didn't work. I couldn't stop it ramming the car that was crossing in front of me."

Sean checked the other car, but the driver was not injured, since Hamish had hit its rear door and trunk.

Hamish was able to get out of his car, feel his torso, legs and arms, and conclude that he was basically unhurt. He said so to the EMT personnel, but they insisted that he get into the ambulance to be checked out at the hospital.

In the meantime, Sean arranged to have Hamish's car towed. He instructed the tow truck driver to take it to the local garage. He asked the owner to see if it could be repaired, and added: "Please find the reason it wouldn't stop."

The answer came back soon enough. One look under the car by the mechanic at the garage was enough to uncover the cause for the crash: a brake line that had been cut. The damage to the front of the Prius was not too serious though, and once they got a new bumper and hood they should be able to repair it.

When he returned from the hospital, with a clean bill of health, Hamish called Joe Washington at the RCMP's Lunenburg detachment and explained to him what had happened. "Now I hope you'll take the threats against me seriously! You can bet the accident was related to those threats."

Sounding both contrite and resentful at the same time, Washington promised to help. "I'll send around a detective to view the car. If it looks like sabotage, I'll try to find out more about the two ex-convicts you mentioned. In the meantime, don't try to do our job for us." He hung up.

15

Intrigue

The police completed their search for clues at 17 Harrow Place and told Olivia that she could move back in. They had dusted for fingerprints and there was still dust over furniture in the dining room, the kitchen, the study, and the bedrooms that were not under renovation.

Olivia began her own examination of her husband's possessions. She wanted to find any information about the nature of Larry's involvement with UModel.ca and evidence of the existence of assets that her lawyer would need to know about when settling his estate. She would have to go to the flat in Halifax to do the same thing there.

The study contained a desk and a filing cabinet which had been used by Rizzo. She found that one drawer of the desk and the filing cabinet were locked, so she went to the bedroom to find his set of keys. One of them fit the locked drawer. Inside were some papers and letters. Some of them involved the purchase and title to 17 Harrow Place, the contract for reno-vations, and the homeowner insurance policy. Another set of documents was on the letterhead of Classy Escort Services, with a Los Angeles address. These seemed to be copies of letters sent by Rizzo, with his signature at the bottom. She looked at the addressees, and saw that one of them was Jerry Farthing. The letter was an invoice for $1,500 "for services rendered." There was another one with a name she recognized. It belonged to a California congressman who had recently been embroiled in a messy divorce. The invoice was dated a dozen years previously.

She found a key in the locked drawer and tried it in the lock of the grey steel filing cabinet. It clicked open. Inside were hanging folders containing information on various models, with personal details. Olivia did not recognize any of the names and did not go through the folders. She opened an unmarked file folder, which contained photographs of Anthony Thompson, with various young women. She put the files back, locked the cabinet and the desk, and put the keys to them on her own keychain.

*****

Superintendent Klijs asked Olivia Rizzo to present herself for questioning once again at the Lunenburg detachment. Olivia came accompanied by her solicitor. Jeffrey Dobbs, QC, was an experienced Halifax lawyer in his sixties who dealt mainly in criminal cases. On their way over, he cautioned Olivia not to answer questions of a substantive nature.

Klijs was waiting for them in the interview room. He was alone but Olivia realized that the interview was being taped so that everything she said would be on the record. She settled into her uncomfortable chair and looked at the RCMP officer.

Klijs started by saying that they had made progress in solving Larry Rizzo's murder. "We are trying to pin down the events on the night of the murder. Mrs. Rizzo, you said that you never made a call to Sean Carroll in the early hours of June 23rd, though he claims that is the reason he went to your home at 17 Harrow Place. We have examined your cell phone and the records for your parents' home phone, and they confirm what you said. However, we have also obtained Mr. Carroll's phone records, and he did indeed receive a phone call at 3:58 am, and the location data show it was made from a place in Old Town near 17 Harrow Place. We do not know who owns that phone, since it was purchased with a prepaid number of minutes on it. Now Mrs. Rizzo, would you tell us what really happened that night? When did you leave the house? And did you talk to him afterwards, or phone Sean Carroll?"

Dobbs raised his hand as if to stop him. "My client has nothing to say at this time."

Klijs was angry, and he glared at Dobbs. "You may regret not cooperating in our investigation. But for now, your client is free to leave."

*****

The RCMP sent a cruiser to arrest Sean Carroll. Joe Washington got out and rapped on the door. He was accompanied by a constable. When Sean answered, he said: "Sean, it pains me to have to arrest you, but you brought it on yourself. Your lack of cooperation made it virtually certain that you would be charged with the murder of Larry Rizzo. I think you've let your heart get in the way of your common sense."

"But I told you all I know!"

Hamish came out and told Sean not to worry, he'd contact a lawyer and get him out on bail. When the police cruiser drove away he called a lawyer friend of his in Halifax and started the process. The judge did not consider Sean a flight risk so he was back at The Oaks the next day.

He and Hamish sat down together over a pot of coffee to discuss the case. Sean admitted he might have been wrong about Olivia: "Someone obviously wanted me to be a suspect for Larry's murder. I don't think Olivia would do that, but I swear it was Olivia's voice on the phone at 4 am."

As they were talking a call came in from Olivia, which Sean picked up. "I've gone through Larry's papers at 17 Harrow Place, and I think they may shed some light on the activities of UModel. Do you want to come over to have a look at them?"

Sean answered coolly, "Sure, Olivia, either Hamish or I will stop by today."

After she had rung off, Hamish gave his view on what they should do: "Sean, I'm going to have to take over investigating this case. You're much too close to it. I'll coordinate with your lawyer, of course."

"I feel I should do something."

"The less you do now, the better. If you weren't obliged to stay put I'd suggest you go off on holiday! Maybe just get some sailing in with your buddies at the yacht club. Or spend some time with Marjoree. You haven't seen her in a while." Marjoree was a strawberry blonde who until Olivia came along was Sean's romantic interest. She lived in one of a row of upscale townhouses newly built in Old Town.

Sean shrugged his shoulders, ``OK, I'll stay away from the case and keep my nose clean."

Hamish nodded his head. "Good. Let me be the one to look through Larry's papers."

16

Hamish

Hamish took the hanging files out of the grey metal cabinet at 17 Harrow Place and spread them on the mahogany desk. There were a dozen of them, each containing pictures of a different female model. He noted two things that they all had in common: the photos were of young women, seemingly no more than twenty years old, and probably less, and they all lived within Nova Scotia, most of them around Halifax. The files gave contact information, but no employment details.

A file with no identifying tab and containing photographs of a man with various young women was more intriguing. Sean had told Hamish about his run-in with one of his classmates and shown him clippings from the *Ashcroft Examiner,* so Hamish recognized Anthony Thompson. Comparing these photos with those in the models' files turned up three matches among his women companions. Hamish took the files with him, relocked the desk and metal cabinet, and left the office. Giving the keys back to Olivia, he told her that he would study the files at the detective agency's office and left via the front door.

Back at The Oaks, Hamish called the phone number of each of the three young women. The first number yielded a recording that the phone was no longer in service. The second call was answered by a female voice. Hamish said: "I would like to speak to Susan Dey about modelling work."

The woman replied: "I don't do that anymore. I have another job now."

"May I ask why? It pays good money."

She hesitated. "Because in my experience it involves more than just modelling. That's all I want to say." She hung up.

Hamish tried the third one, and was connected to the person named in the file. Again he implied that he wanted to offer her a modelling job. The woman replied: "Who's it with? I don't work for just anybody. And none of that bullshit about looking for a new face to launch a new product line. I fell for that once and once is enough."

Hamish decided to come clean. "Actually, I'm a detective investigating the death of someone in the modelling business, Larry Rizzo. Did you know him?"

"Oh, Larry. I had no idea he had died, but then I don't read the papers or watch the TV news. So, what does that have to do with me?"

"I found your file in Larry's home office. Since UModel.ca has complete files of all the models who got jobs through them at the Halifax office, I'm guessing that there's something significant about you and a few others. Can I come to talk to you about your modelling experience?"

There was a pause, then she said: "OK, you could meet me at 5:30 pm tomorrow at a cafe near where I work in Halifax. I have a job as an office receptionist now. It's on Young Street."

*****

Hamish pushed the door of the cafe at the address he was given. He thought he recognized the woman from the photo in the file, though she looked a bit older now. She was tall and thin, with high cheekbones and a mane of red hair. He went over and asked her: "Are you Karen Swisher?"

"Yes, you must be Hamish. What would you like to know?"

"I'd like to know what happened when you posted on UModel.ca. I assume that's how you got your modelling jobs?"

"That's right. I was still in high school and I was attracted by the glamour of fashion modelling, so I put my bio and a few photos up on UModel, without telling my parents. I got a call almost right away, and I went into Halifax for an interview. My parents live on the outskirts so going to the big city was an adventure for me."

"Was Larry Rizzo one of those who interviewed you?"

"No, there were two men, Andy Something and Anthony Thompson. They said I had the possibility of a top modelling career ahead of me because of a great opportunity that had just come up. Thompson told me that I would need a proper portfolio of pictures but he could do that for me, he would arrange for a photographer to meet us at his studio. But it turned out that it was a studio apartment and there were just the two of us. He grabbed me and tried to undress me, but I resisted. I was able to get away from him, run out the door of his apartment and dash down the stairs to the street."

"So did you call the police?"

"No, what was the use? My word against that of a rich patron of the arts who is involved with a number of charities? I looked him up later on the internet. As soon as I got home I took my post off UModel and never had anything else to do with them. The whole thing soured me on modelling, though I'm thinking of getting back into it, with a reputable agency. At least I have my eyes open now."

"So this Andy fellow was part of scam to lure young woman into sex?"

"Yes, I'm sure of that. He gave me the pitch that led me to go to Thompson's apartment."

"What about Rizzo? Did you have any dealings with him?"

"No, not really. But after I took my photos off their website he contacted me to ask why."

"Did you tell him what happened?"

"Not in so many words. But I made it clear that I didn't want to have anything to do with Thompson or UModel again."

*****

It was a nice mid-summer day as Hamish drove back to Ashcroft along Route 5. The sun was out, and there was warmth in the air. On impulse, he stopped at the site of the New Dawn retirement home where he had lived two years before. The building had disappeared, the burnt-out hulk having been demolished and even the concrete slab on which it had rested broken up and carted away.

He parked just off the road. The winding driveway had a chain across it, with a sign that said "Do Not Enter. Private Property." Hamish understood that the property now belonged to the town, having been seized for nonpayment of taxes. New Dawn's owners, Jerry Adams and Guy Laframboise, were in jail, thanks to the efforts of Hamish and Sean.

He walked up to the place where the main building had stood. The view over Trahearne Bay was still breathtaking, even though the flower beds that had been so beautiful were no longer planted and the bushes and trees were left untended. At least the town would occasionally mow the lawn.

Hamish looked over toward the Taramichi River and could see the Strathcona Clinic in the foreground, nestled among the trees. Hamish recalled the frightening experience of being sent there when he was thought to have had a stroke, and later when he and Sean returned to accuse the head doctor, Art Gibson, of fraud. Gibson had also gone to jail. The clinic was still in operation, but under different management.

An outbuilding remained on the New Dawn site, though it showed no signs of having been used since the fire that destroyed the residence. Hamish thought it had served as staff quarters. He tried the door, but it was locked.

On his way back to his car, he took a detour along the edge of the lawn, beside the woods that surrounded the property. He remembered a path that wound its way through the trees down to Trahearne Bay, a good kilometre away. He had often taken advantage of good weather to walk to the water through the woods when he lived at New Dawn. This had been one of his favourite places.

He looked down the path, which was now overgrown, and decided not to try to push his way through the bushes. He saw two deer in a field a few hundred metres away, munching on the leaves of a sapling. The woodsy smells took him back to some of the happy days he had spent here, so he paused to take several more breaths, content to be here once again.

About to head back, he noticed that there was a mound of earth that appeared to have been dug up recently, perhaps by a dog or a fox. Leaning over to look more closely, he saw something in a hole beside the pile of dirt. It was a badly decomposed human hand. Hamish took out his cellphone and called Joe Washington.

Hamish waited by the road for the RCMP team to arrive, and then showed them the location of the human remains. A police constable examined the area around it for clues while the medical examiner gingerly removed dirt around the rest of the body. Hamish was asked to leave so as not to further contaminate the site, and he got into his car and returned to The Oaks.

*****

Hamish decided to call the other women with their files in Rizzo's office. Of the nine others, three were no longer reachable at the phone number given in their file, and in four cases he was connected to voicemail. He left a message that he was calling about modelling opportunities. Of his remaining calls, two were picked up, the first by the model's mother. When she heard that Hamish wanted to discuss modelling she started swearing a blue streak. "I don't ever want you or the other sons-of-bitches at UModel to call her again! The business is just a front for prostitution!"

Hamish managed to get her to accept that he was investigating the modelling internet site and did not work for UModel, but the woman was reluctant to give any details of her daughter's experience.

"Can you tell me who she dealt with at UModel?"

"I don't remember exactly. Tell you what, I'll ask her and if I get anything useful out of her, I'll call you."

"Is she still modelling?"

"No, the bloom is off the rose, as far as she's concerned. As for me, I only agreed to it at the time because she swore that UModel was a reputable modelling agency. Fat chance of that!"

The final call was answered by the model herself, who was quite willing to discuss her experience with UModel, which was five years previous. "I had hired a professional photographer to put together a portfolio, and I posted it at UModel and on another modelling website. I took a job with an ad agency through the latter, doing publicity for a local car dealer. Then Andy Leipzig phoned me and spun a yarn about a special client wanting to interview me in person. I was wary, but I went to meet him at a local restaurant anyway. When I saw that he wanted to hit on me I just got up and left. I took my portfolio off the UModel website right after that."

"Do you remember the name of the man you met at the restaurant?"

"It was Jerry somebody."

"Jerry Farthing?"

"Yeah, that's it."

Hamish thanked her for her time, then remembered another question: "What about Larry Rizzo? Ever meet with him?"

"No, I don't know anyone by that name."

*****

After hanging up, Hamish immediately got another call that was waiting on the line. Joe Washington, sounding more solicitous now, said: "Hamish, we did confirm that your brake line had been cut. And we are looking into the activities of Clement Benedict. The force has searched his flat in Halifax, and there are a lot of clippings from newspapers concerning you. Nothing conclusive, though. I suggest being careful, not opening the door to strangers or going out unaccompanied. Perhaps also getting the use of a different car that can't be so easily identified with you."

"Thanks for the advice. I'd also like you to know that Larry Rizzo seemed to have suspicions about others associated with UModel, namely that they were using it to lure young women, and perhaps girls, for sex. This could well have been the reason he was murdered. Have you investigated this?"

Sounding huffy, Joe Washington replied: "I can't tell you about our investigations, but I can assure you that we will leave no stone unturned." He said goodbye and hung up.

17

Los Angeles, the 1990's

Larry was only a little more than a year out of high school, and now he was on his own. The breakup with Olivia was a blow to his self-confidence, and being told by his parents to get out of town was even worse. His father said to him: "We don't want to see your pretty face anymore. I sure as hell don't want the cops breathing down my neck. Just beat it."

Even his mother didn't stand up for him. So he crammed his things into a backpack and hitched his way along the Trans-Canada until he got to Winnipeg. There he met a girl who said she had a friend in Los Angeles who could put her up until she found a job in the movie business. She had an old Plymouth and she offered him a ride if he did his share of the driving.

In four days they were in LA. The girl dropped him off in a seedy part of town where he rented a room and tried to find an angle that would allow him to earn some money. This proved to be harder than he'd thought and he was forced to take any menial job that was on offer.

The first few years of his life in LA were tough. He started by running errands for small-time gangsters, and ripping off tourists with promises to show them the hideouts of film stars. When they paid him for the tour he disappeared. For a while he pimped for a woman he had run into on the street. Linda Lace was her working name. She was plump, sexy, and funny at the same time. They made a good team, until her heroin habit made her lose interest in dressing up and minding her personal hygiene. Larry dumped her then.

He kicked around LA for a while before he came up with the idea of starting an escort service. His brief stint as a pimp had shown him how big the market was for sex. He decided that high class prostitution was where the money was, a great opportunity that was not yet fully exploited in town. Not only were there hordes of horny male visitors looking to meet glamorous women who were, or might become, Hollywood stars, there were also a lot of young women hoping to become movie stars who needed to make a living while they waited for their big break. Some worked as models, others as call girls.

So Larry printed up some business cards for Classy Escort Services and put an advert in the *LA Times*. Almost immediately, he received half a dozen applications from women wanting to do the escort job. Given the number of applicants, Larry could afford to be choosy, since his goal was to manage just two escorts initially. He rented a suite at a nearby Holiday Inn and scheduled the applicants to show up at 15 minute intervals. Of the six, he chose two women who seemed to have extroverted personalities, good figures, and a distinguished bearing. It turned out that both Mandy and Natasha did a little modelling, and their agent happened to be Andy Leipzig. The two women were in their mid-twenties, and had come to LA from the Midwest with hopes of getting into motion pictures.

It was in the women's interest not to reveal to Andy that they were moonlighting as escorts, and Larry also steered clear of him, at least initially. Andy for his part was a small-time fashion modelling agent. He did not deal with the advertising companies or movie studios themselves, but just located talent and steered them to the established talent agencies, for a fee.

A chance encounter brought Larry and Andy together. A client phoned Larry with a request to hire Natasha, whom he knew from a previous business trip to LA. Larry tried calling her cell, without success, so he went down the list of her other contact numbers. When a man picked up the phone, Larry said to him that someone urgently wanted to hire Natasha. Andy, suspecting that the call was a big modelling agency, demanded his cut. Larry was forced to explain the nature of the work, namely that she was being hired to be an escort.

Andy for his part had also seen the advantages of marketing women both as models and as escorts. Of course, women who were successful models wouldn't want to have anything to do with the likes of him, but those who were struggling could at least keep alive their dream while making enough on the side to live on. He suggested to Larry that they get together to consider the advantages of combining the two operations.

The two men met at the Black Cat Cafe to talk things over. At first, neither was very impressed by the other. Leipzig looked like a down-at-heels accountant, with a receding hairline, worn trousers, and a white shirt. Rizzo was more handsome, with wavy black hair and a well-proportioned face, but he wore a leather jacket and looked like the small-time crook that he was. Nevertheless, they quickly saw that they were on the same wavelength and would benefit from working together. It was clear that Andy had skills as an organizer, while Larry had the charm of a salesman who could attract the clients and deal with the concerns of the women working as escorts. Andy agreed to make some of his other models available to Larry's escort service, in exchange for a share of the profits. They would become partners in Classy Escort Services.

Both of them realized that making a serious profit involved creating a high-class operation, and that required money. They needed to hire limos to ferry around the escorts and their clients and pay the women well so that they could afford elegant clothes. They also needed to attract a rich clientele by paying doormen and concierges at the better hotels to steer business their way. But neither Larry nor Andy had any capital.

They got lucky when one of their clients turned out to be Jerry Farthing. He hired Mandy to accompany him during a two-day visit to LA to meet with investors in a venture-capital firm that he had just founded. Afterwards, he approached Rizzo and Leipzig with a proposition: make me a partner and I'll finance a much classier operation which will be profitable for the three of us. They agreed. With Farthing's cash they leased two limos and hired more women. They offered to meet clients at the airport and ferry them, with their escorts, to downtown hotels. At Farthing's insistence, they hired a few younger women, even underage ones, though they were careful not to advertise the fact. In just a few months, Classy Escort Services became one of the most successful and reputed escort agencies in LA.

For the first time in his life, Larry had more money than he knew how to spend. He bought himself expensive cars, and invested in real estate. He became known as a successful entrepreneur, and he started mixing with the movers and shakers in town. Larry was careful to keep records of the customers of the escort service, just in case they became famous and he could tap them for some money or get them to do favours for him. This proved to be a useful sidelight.

However, success bred competition, and soon other firms sprang up that offered the same services. Some of them moreover had the ear of politicians who were promising to clean up the city. Suddenly Classy Escort Services was in their crosshairs. Running the business became less profitable. The firm now had to pay bribes to crooked policemen and politicians to avoid being closed down. And with other companies getting into the same business it was no longer a seller's market.

At the same time, Jerry Farthing was having his troubles with prosecutors in New York City, following complaints that he was luring teenage girls to his penthouse apartment. He considered moving his investment business to California, but decided instead that relocating to Canada might be a safer option for escaping from the New York prosecutors' oversight. Larry convinced him of the attractions of Nova Scotia for someone with Jerry's tastes. Farthing had already collaborated with

Anthony Thompson in providing cross-border financing so he had contacts in Halifax, including in the theatre business. They shared a fondness for young women, the younger the better.

Thus Larry, Andy, and Jerry conceived a plan to move their operations to Halifax. Andy was aware of job placement websites for models, and he and Larry had created a fledgling company called UModel.com that was just getting off the ground in the United States. They decided to close their LA escort service, sell their interest in UModel.com, and devote their energies to starting a Canadian internet-based modelling company, the on-line platform UModel.ca. Anthony Thompson readily agreed to Farthing's request to provide some of the financing to get the Canadian business up and running. Larry and Andy sold the US operation to some of their associates and moved to Halifax.

Rizzo was wary of having anything to do with Thompson, remembering their bitter rivalry in high school. However, he went along with the plans for UModel.ca, vowing to find a way to get back at his enemy on his own turf.

18

Sean

Sean went back to talk to his friend Terry, at the Ashcroft *Examiner's* office. He couldn't sit still and let others work on the case, despite Hamish's advice. It was like an itch which he knew he shouldn't scratch, but that he couldn't stop himself from doing.

"Terry, I know that you hear about things that you don't publish in the paper because they can't be confirmed. Have there been any rumours about men using a modelling agency to lure young women for sex? It might involve Larry Rizzo's outfit, UModel.ca, and could be the reason that he was shot."

"They're located in Halifax, aren't they? That's really outside my usual beat. I did hear about the party that the fellow from New York I told you about held a few nights ago in what used to be the Wildman mansion. I sent a reporter who does the society column out there to cover it, but the owner, Jerry Farthing, declined to be photographed. That's a first in my experience! So

I did a little research on him and it turns out that he signed a consent decree with a prosecutor in New York City not to entertain minors, in response to an accusation that he was an accessory to the procurement of under-age women."

"Interesting. Perhaps that's the reason he bought a summer place up here in Nova Scotia, outside the reach of New York law enforcement. And Larry Rizzo, any rumours about him?"

"Not really. After his return to Nova Scotia he spent most of his time in Halifax, so he was not much involved with life here. His family no longer lives here either. His parents are dead, and his siblings have all moved away. Their old house has been demolished. We did an article about Larry after he bought the old mansion here on Harrow Place. You know, 'local boy makes good,' that sort of thing. We included a few photos. One thing we didn't mention was that there was some issue about his purchase of the house. The funds were supposed to be wired up from New York, but there was a hitch and the purchase was delayed by a few weeks. I never knew why, and in any case it all got sorted out."

*****

Sean stopped by the townhouse where Marjoree Price lived. She hadn't seen him in some time, and he knew he would have to make amends, so he brought her a bouquet of red roses. She opened the door and led him into her opulently furnished living room. There were abstract paintings on the wall, and the furniture was made of glass and stainless steel. Area rugs covered part of the floor made of red oak planks. She invited him to sit on the couch next to her.

"Well Sean, I wondered if you would ever show up again! What have you been up to? I did see in the *Examiner* that you had discovered the body of your old girlfriend's husband. At least you're not behind bars!"

"She's not my old girlfriend, just a long-ago classmate. And yes, I am under suspicion of not being truthful with the police, even though I told them everything I know, which unfortunately is very little. Hamish has ordered me not to get involved, but I feel I have to find out what actually happened."

"Why don't you just chill out? Let's borrow your friend's sailboat and anchor in a cove off Trahearne Bay, have a nice lunch and sail back. That would be fun!"

Sean looked doubtful. "Tell me, do you know Anthony Thompson? I think he has a townhouse nearby."

Marjoree had bought her two-bedroom townhouse when her New Dawn retirement residence, where she had met Sean and Hamish, had burned down. She had enjoyed not having to worry about preparing meals and arranging for maintenance at New Dawn, but had adjusted happily to owning her own home once again. "Yes, he's part of this same development. I see him occasionally driving his Ferrari around with one or another young woman in the passenger seat. I swear that some of them seem to be about 15 -- though that may be because at my age I can't distinguish 15 from 25!" She laughed.

"Have you ever seen him with Larry Rizzo's wife Olivia?"

"Oh, you mean your heartthrob? I don't know her, but I did see him once with a woman about his age, elegantly dressed in very nice and expensive clothes. This was a few weeks ago. They were talking animatedly on the sidewalk before he unlocked his front door. Then they both went inside."

"You're sure of that? That was about the time of the class reunion. I saw Olivia at the reunion and she hired me to investigate her husband. Anthony Thompson was also there, but not her husband."

"Well, if that was her, it seems that maybe she was already doing some investigating!"

Sean frowned. "Actually, it was her husband's business activities that she wanted me to look into."

Marjoree teased him. "Well, you know men. Always happy to mix business with pleasure!"

They chatted a few minutes longer, and Sean gave excuses for not being able to sail with her. "I have to go to Halifax. I think the key to this mystery lies with the UModel office there. Until I talk to Larry Rizzo's sidekick, Andy Leipzig, I won't be able to understand what Larry's role in the business was. I haven't been able to make an appointment to see him, so I'll just have to barge in there and hope to find him in the office."

"Be careful! I think you're making a mistake. Leave the investigating to Hamish and the RCMP."

"I can't. I'm going to go crazy if I just sit on my hands."

*****

When Sean entered the modelling agency the receptionist was once again typing behind the window in the inner office. She did not indicate that she remembered who he was, but asked: "What can I do for you?"

Sean impatiently explained that he had been waiting a week for her to book a new appointment with Mr. Leipzig, but he had heard nothing and had decided to return anyway. "I really need to talk to him!"

The receptionist said impassively: "I'll see if he's available."

She picked up the phone and said: "A Mr. Carroll to see you, Andy." After listening for a moment, she turned to Sean and said: "He'll be out in a few minutes."

A quarter of an hour later the door to an inner office opened and a man of average height and balding head emerged, wearing a dress shirt and slacks. The shirt was unbuttoned at the top, revealing a gold chain around his neck. He stuck out his hand and said, in a neutral voice: "I'm Andy Leipzig. What can I do for you?"

Sean explained that he was assisting Olivia Lopes' lawyer in tracking down the elements of Larry Rizzo's estate.

Leipzig shrugged. "I've already given all the information I have to Larry Rizzo's widow. Just tell Olivia's lawyer to contact my office if he needs something more."

In the face of this stonewalling, Sean decided to be more aggressive. "I'd like to know more about how this office operates, and Larry Rizzo's role in it. Thanks to UModel, a young woman was lured to a party given by Jerry Farthing last Saturday, and invited to pose nude. Apparently you were at the party too. Is this the way you do business?"

Leipzig drew himself up to his full height of 5 foot, 10 inches. "We are just a middleman between potential models and employers. We are not responsible for the behaviour of either."

"But your website says that you vet your clients to make sure that they are on the level. If they are not, then you're guilty of abetting their criminal behaviour."

Leipzig grew angry. "That's enough! I have nothing further to say to you." He stormed back into his office and slammed the door.

The receptionist gave Sean a sardonic grin. "Well, you got your face-to-face meeting with Mr. Leipzig, so I won't need to make an appointment for you." She went back to her typing and did not look up when he went out the door.

*****

When Sean got back to The Oaks he found a message from Joe Washington to call him. Hamish wanted to talk to Sean first. "You've been sleuthing Larry Rizzo's murder, which you shouldn't be doing. You're going to get into more trouble!"

Joe Washington confirmed this. "Robert Klijs has informed me that you contacted an associate of Larry Rizzo and hence someone who may well be asked to testify to events leading up to his murder. I explicitly told you not to do any investigating on your own. You're putting yourself at risk of a charge of witness tampering. Don't forget that you're still under investigation for Rizzo's murder."

After Washington hung up, Sean sat down with Hamish in the detective agency's conference room to discuss the case. Hamish started by saying: "I don't think you should even be told what facts I turn up or what theories seem to me most plausible. But I can see that you're going to try to find out for yourself if I keep you in the dark."

Hamish paused, then said: "I suspect that the RCMP have put together a list of suspects that includes Olivia, Andy Leipzig and you. Olivia is the obvious one, given reports of marital difficulties, but she has an alibi. Leipzig would benefit from Rizzo's death because the partnership agreement gives the business to him. And you, Sean, were the one found at the site of the murder. You could have been lured by Olivia to get rid of her husband."

Sean moved to protest, but Hamish ignored him and continued: "The thing I don't know is whether Joe Washington and company are investigating UModel and have learned about its role in procuring under-age women for Jerry Farthing and Anthony Thompson. Those two might have had a motive to kill Rizzo also, if Rizzo was aware of what was going on. The big unknown is the nature of Rizzo's involvement. Was he a participant in the scheme or instead did he attempt to stop it? Perhaps he was blackmailing those involved. We need to look into his financial records, and also interview more of the models. But it will have to be me who does it -- you can't afford to be seen doing any sleuthing, if you want to stay out of jail."

"But I have an advantage over you; I know the people involved, going as far back as high school. And I suspect that understanding their motivations is as important as digging up incriminating facts."

"We'll see about that. So, what are your suspicions about what happened?"

"I don't believe that Larry Rizzo participated in a procurement ring, nor do I think that Olivia had anything to do with his death. But I agree that we need to know more about what Farthing and Thompson were up to. How many girls did they lure to their place, and what happened to them? So far, we've only spoken to those who got away. Did they kidnap others? We need the help of the police to see if there are some missing teenagers who might have been abducted by them. And we need to know Andy Leipzig's role in all of this."

Hamish nodded thoughtfully. "We can only hope that they're looking into the procurement angle, but I don't have much confidence that they are, even though I brought it to Joe Washington's attention. We'll need to get some evidence before they take me seriously and do something about it. I'm going to start by trying to contact some of the other women in Larry Rizzo's files."

19

The Women

Hamish had left voicemail for four women, but none of them had called him back. He called them again, leaving a more explicit message: "I am investigating the operations of UModel, and would like you to describe your experience, in confidence."

Almost right away, he received a call back. A woman with a husky voice identified herself as Natalie Short. "What would you like to know, and what do you intend to do with the information?"

"Can you tell me who you dealt with at UModel, and whether this led to a job in modelling?" Hamish explained that there had been a murder of one of the principals of UModel, and he was trying to discover if was related to the modelling website.

"A murder! I had no idea! In any case I never met anyone with that name, and I didn't know there was someone called Larry Rizzo who was associated with UModel."

"Were you interviewed for a modelling position? If so, by whom?"

"I was called by a Mr. Leipzig, and asked to show up for an interview in Halifax at one of the big hotels. I went up to the suite he indicated, thinking that I would be in a room with other candidates waiting to be interviewed, but I was the only one there. The door was opened by a middle-aged man, who said he was Jerry, but didn't give his last name. He explained that they needed a model to pose in swimwear. After looking through my portfolio he said that he thought I would be a good candidate but that first he would need to see me undressed. I was gullible and only 15 at the time, so I did as he requested. He told me that I would be perfect for the position, but then he started to touch me and I realized what this was all about. I hastily pulled on my clothes and got out of there."

"Did you tell anyone about this?"

"No, I was too ashamed, and I didn't want my parents to know what I'd done. I'd posted my photos on UModel as a lark, without telling them. After my so-called interview I removed my post and gave up my dream of becoming a model."

"What do you do now?"

"I'm at university, studying science at EU. I hope to go on to a postgraduate degree in health care."

"Would you be willing to tell the RCMP what you told me? We need them to put a stop to the type of thing that happened to you. There are others who had a similar experience. You might want to join them in a civil suit to get compensation from UModel and the man who molested you."

"I'd like to think it over first, and perhaps consult a lawyer."

"OK, we can leave it at that for now. I'll get back in touch."

*****

Sean got a call from his niece, Kimberly Weedon. "Sophie's still keen to go undercover and apply to UModel for a job. Her parents have apparently said yes, though I don't know if they are truly aware of just what I went through."

"I'd better talk to them first."

Sean called the home number of Sophie's parents, John and Marie Strassen. "This could be dangerous for Sophie, but I'll be nearby, monitoring my phone and prepared to intervene if necessary."

John Strassen didn't seem overly concerned. "Sophie's pretty good at taking care of herself, and if you think this could help prevent other girls getting lured into prostitution, then we'll let her do it! But what about the RCMP? Shouldn't they be brought into it?"

"I'll contact them and explain the situation. I'll try to get them to be on standby."

*****

Hamish did some more research on the girl whose phone number had been removed from service, Carrie Laporta. He Googled the name, and two news stories came up. Carrie, it turned out, had been reported missing by her parents. She was a wild teenager, and they suspected that she had run away from her home on Cape Breton. A subsequent story reported that she was still missing and that the police had found no trace of her.

When Hamish called Joe Washington to discuss assistance in collecting evidence of wrongdoing by UModel, he was again strongly advised not to attempt to do police work. "Moreover,"

Joe explained, "if you record a conversation without permission you are guilty of violation of privacy."

Hamish replied in an exasperated tone: "I'm aware of that. I'm a former judge, after all! As for UModel, I've discovered that one girl who posted on their internet site has disappeared, Carrie Laporta. I wonder if there's a connection."

"OK, I'll have someone check that out. Thanks for the tip. We are looking into the activities of UModel, but so far have found nothing illegal nor any connection with the murder of Larry Rizzo. However, our investigation is continuing."

In the meantime Sean heard from Kimberly that Sophie had decided to proceed with her plan to post information on UModel and see if Leipzig and Farthing took the bait. Her father, John Strassen had given his permission despite having been warned that the RCMP might not be directly involved. He told Sean: "Her judo training may well come in handy. You know she's a brown belt already!"

Sean called Sophie to try to talk her out of it, but she was determined. "I think those men are awful. If I can get them put away, then it will have been worth it!"

"OK then, but be careful! I'll try to be close by if you need help." Sean gave her two phone numbers to call in case of an emergency, and wished her good luck.

A few days later Sophie was invited for an interview at the UModel office on Connaught Avenue at 2 pm. Sean drove to Windsor, picked Sophie up, and drove her to UModel. He waited outside in his car while she went up to the third floor. The office was empty, except for the woman in the inner office, who was busy entering information into her computer. She looked up as Sophie entered, and said: "Can I help you?"

"I'm here for a modelling appointment."

"You're Sophie Evans? There's been a change in plans. Your interview is going to be at another location, and a driver is on his way here to pick you up."

"What location -- is it far?"

"It's on the South Shore, about 30 minutes away."

"I'll have to call my parents to let them know. May I have the address, please?"

Sophie in fact called Sean to give him the address. He recognized that it was the Wildman mansion, the place where Kimberly was taken, and he said so to Sophie. He asked her: "Are you sure you want to do this? You remember what happened to Kimberly."

"It's OK, I'll be fine." She turned to the receptionist: "Will I be driven back here, and how long will it take?"

"I don't know for sure, but I expect you'll be back in Halifax by 5 pm. The chauffeur can drop you wherever you like."

She passed on the information to Sean, who said: "OK then. Call or text me if you need my help."

A few minutes later Gus entered the office, and introduced himself to Sophie as an assistant to the person who could launch her modelling career if she impressed him favourably. "He works with all the big agencies in New York. He's too busy to come up to Halifax today but he's looked at your file and thinks you might be just the right model for a new line of young women's lingerie. If you impress him then he will recommend you for the job."

Sophie giggled excitedly and pretended to be taken in by the story. "OK, let's go!"

They took the elevator down to the parking garage, where Gus opened a rear door of the Town Car for her. They drove off, and as they emerged from the ramp into the street, she noticed that Sean's car was no longer there.

The traffic was light and half an hour later the limo turned up the driveway to Jerry Farthing's house. Instead of going to the front door, Gus drove into the garage and took Sophie around to the back of the house, opening the sliding glass doors from the patio and inviting her into a lounge with a camera tripod in the middle. Sophie looked around and recognized the room that Kimberly had described.

"If you would wait here a few minutes, Mr. Farthing will be right with you. Can I get you something to drink?"

"Actually, no, but could I use the washroom?"

Gus pointed to a closed door on the far side of the room. "It's right through there." He left by another door at the opposite end of the room.

The washroom was the size of a closet, and contained only the toilet and a small sink with a mirror over it. After locking the door, Sophie called Sean. "I'm in the back room, accessible from the patio. I haven't met Farthing yet. That's all for now."

After touching up her makeup, she re-emerged just as a gentleman with grey hair entered the room. He said: "Hello, I'm Jerry. How are you Sophie? You must be tired after your long drive. Let me fix you a drink." He walked over to what looked like an entertainment centre, sliding open what turned out to be a fridge. "How about a coke with a little rum in it?" When Sophie did not refuse, he poured something in a tall glass containing Coca Cola and stirred it with a swizzle stick. He handed it to her and poured himself a drink from a bottle labelled Bowmore Single Malt.

Sophie did not want to drink it but the man was staring at her so she took a little sip. There was a faint taste of liquor but not too strong. She had tried spirits before, however, and knew to be wary of their delayed effect, so she didn't drink any more. She was already starting to feel a little woozy. *There must be more in it than rum,* she thought with a sense of panic.

"Is it good?" her host asked, and she smiled and said yes, playing along with him. When he turned away to pick up his own drink, she poured a little of her glass into a vase containing half a dozen red roses.

He smiled at her, as he greedily looked her up and down. "It's good of you to agree to come here. I can see now that you are just the person we are looking for! And I don't think you will be disappointed. Are you interested in an exciting career in modelling? You could wear all sorts of glamorous clothes, travel to New York, Paris, London, … I can make that happen for you. What do you say?"

Sophie nodded enthusiastically. At the same time, she was starting to feel vaguely sleepy, and Jerry's face was becoming a little blurry. She fought to focus on him. "What do I have to do?" she asked.

Jerry got up and went to a shelf in a corner of the room, pulling out a flat box, which he opened, and removing a bra and panties. "First you need to put on this lingerie and we'll take a few pictures. I'll send them on to the modelling agency in New

York, and we'll go from there. You can use the powder room to change." He handed her the lingerie.

She walked a little unsteadily back to the washroom and locked the door. She still had her phone, but knew that she would have to leave it there after changing out of her clothes. She texted Sean: "I've been asked to put on lingerie, and I think my drink was drugged."

Jerry called to her impatiently from the other room: "What's taking so long Sophie? Do you need help?"

"I won't be a minute!" Sophie undressed, then pulled on the lingerie. It was very skimpy, with the panties no more than a thong and a transparent bra that clearly showed her nipples. Feeling embarrassed, she opened the door and walked back out into the room.

"Let me have a look at you. Good, good, I'm sure the ad agency is going to agree with me that you are perfect for the job. I'll just take a few pictures."

He took out his phone, and took one of her standing in front of him. "We'll need some other poses." He took her by the arm and sat her down on the couch. "Just lie back, and gaze into the camera." He took several more photos.

Sophie was feeling uncomfortable but forced herself to go along with this. But when he tried to get her to take a more alluring pose and he brushed her breast, she slapped his hand away.

"Oh, sorry!" he said. "But you're really very seductive."

She was sitting on the couch and he was next to her. He put his arm around her waist and tried to pull her toward him. Sophie resisted, but realized that her limbs had been weakened by the drink she had tried, even though it was just a small sip. Desperately trying to get away from him, she managed to stand up. When he tried to grab her again she landed a judo kick in his groin. He grunted in pain but he seemed to redouble his efforts, like a wounded bear. He made another lunge for her. She felt her strength give out, and she fell to the floor.

As she did so, the sliding patio door slammed open. Sean stormed in, shouting to Jerry Farthing: "Keep your hands off her, you pig!" When Jerry fell back, startled, Sean took a photo as evidence. It showed both Sophie and Farthing in poses that made clear the nature of their encounter.

Sean said to Sophie: "Quick, get your clothes on, we're leaving!" She went into the powder room to retrieve them. In the meantime, Sean stood over Jerry with a sneer on his face, as if daring him to try to get up. "How many girls have you done this to? You deserve to be locked up, and you will be when the RCMP get here."

Sophie emerged from the powder room fully dressed, and Sean was about to escort her out the patio door when the door from the hallway burst open and Gus walked in. He was holding a pistol in his left hand. Glaring at them, he motioned to Sean and Sophie to stay where they were.

Turning to Farthing, he said: "I heard the ruckus, boss, and I knew there'd be trouble when I found this guy's car nearby. What shall I do with them?"

Farthing's expression had changed from fear to an evil smile. "I'll put the girl in the room over the garage. As for the man, you'll know what to do with the meddling son-of-a-bitch."

He sneered at Sean: "Hey, I recognize you now. You're the guy who came around with a phony story about a car accident. Well, well. It's poetic justice that you're going to die in an automobile crash!"

Gus came over and used a plastic wire tie to fasten Sean's hands behind his back, then shoved him out the door. He said to Farthing: "We'll use his car, which was parked up the road. I'll take him for a little ride in it." He gave a nasty laugh. Pointing his gun at Sean, he motioned him down the driveway towards the highway.

Jerry snarled at Sophie. "We'll resume our fun later. For now, I'm going to lock you up in your room. Walk in front of me up those stairs."

Sophie hung her head dejectedly, apparently docile and drained of energy. *I'll play along for now, until I see an opportunity to escape.* She said to him, "I don't feel well. Can I sit down for a moment?" She moved toward the couch.

"I guess so. You're too heavy for me to carry up the stairs. But just for a minute or two. Here, I'll get you a glass of water." He leered at her, then walked to the wet bar and filled a glass from the tap.

Sophie quickly looked around the room for a weapon. She spotted the camera tripod and slid along the couch toward it. Its legs were constructed of telescoping aluminum tubes but the platform made for a camera to rest on was a heavy block of wood. Jerry turned around and headed back toward Sophie, carrying the glass of water. When he got close he offered the glass to her with his left hand while he ran his right hand down her torso to her waist. The small amount of her drink that

Sophie had consumed was starting to wear off. Instead of taking the glass, she knocked it into his face, causing him to recoil and wipe his eyes. He swore. "You little vixen! You'll pay for this!"

Before he could grab her, Sophie picked up the tripod by one of its legs and swung it around, hitting him just below the knees. He went down, and as he struggled to get up she hit him again, smashing his head with the wood block at the top of the tripod and knocking him out.

Though she thought that he was not going to regain consciousness any time soon, to be safe she used the electric cord of a table lamp to bind his legs together and to tie his arms behind his back. Then she called the other number that Sean had given her.

*****

Gus poked Sean in the back with his gun. "We're going back to your car. So you're a private dick. Not very good at your job, are you?" He spat. When they got to the road they walked a hundred metres beyond the house, where Sean had parked his Subaru in a little layby that partially sheltered it from sight from the house. Gus patted Sean's pockets, reaching into one of them and pulling out a set of keys. He unlocked the car and opened the passenger door, pushing Sean onto the seat before closing the door. He walked around to the driver's side, got in and started the car.

They took a side road that followed the coastline closely and which had been bypassed when the main road was built. There was no traffic. After driving for half a kilometre they stopped at an overlook that had two parking spots, both empty. Gus parked the car near the edge of a cliff. A rickety wooden fence was the only barrier between the tarmac and a rocky precipice that plunged down to the sea.

Gus got out of the car and walked around to the passenger side. "OK, asshole. Now you're going to take your place in the driver's seat." He pulled Sean out of the car and used a pocket knife to cut the wire tie that bound Sean's hands behind his back, while holding the gun in his left hand. Sean hesitated, rubbing his wrists and looking around for a way to escape. He noticed an osprey circling overhead. *I wonder what it sees. Does it consider me dead meat?*

"Get on with it! Don't even think of running," Gus growled. He poked him with the gun. Resigned to his fate, Sean walked around the car and got in on the left side.

Sean didn't see the blow coming. He felt a second of intense pain to the back of his head from the butt of the gun before losing consciousness.

*****

A few minutes earlier, Hamish was peering at the screen of his smartphone, watching the white dot moving along the map. Sean's car had a transmitter that reported its position to the Globalstar satellite network, so that the app on Hamish's phone was able to display its location. Hamish was driving on the same deserted road as Sean's car, but approaching from the other direction. Sophie had told him that Sean had been kidnapped and that Gus intended to kill him in a simulated accident. Hamish fretted. *Come on, come on, I've got to get there before he carries out his plan.*

Trying desperately to keep his eyes both on the road and on his cellphone, he accelerated. Then he noticed the dot was now stationary and only half a kilometre or so ahead, so he slowed down again. Rounding the next bend he saw Sean's Subaru parked at the lookout. Someone was kneeling beside the driver's side door, apparently fiddling with the accelerator or brake pedal. He looked up as Hamish entered the layby. He stood up and reached into his pants pocket.

Hamish felt a mixture of panic and fear. *It looks as if Gus is about to send Sean over the cliff. I've got to do something quickly, but he has a gun!* The gun went off, and Hamish heard the smack of a bullet going through his windshield and a hiss as it went by his head. He was still 10 metres from the man, but the parking area was too narrow for him to turn around. If he tried to stop and back up, he would be an easy target. Without any good alternative, Hamish kept going toward the man with the gun. Another gunshot hit the hood of his Prius, making a zinging noise as it ricocheted off. A second later Hamish hit the man head on. Hamish's car rammed the open driver's side door of Sean's Subaru, ripping it off its hinges. Both the door and Gus were swept over the wood fence and onto the rocks below.

Hamish slammed on the brakes to stop his car, just in time to avoid going over the cliff himself. But the impact had put in motion Sean's car, which was now slowly moving forward. Cursing his shaking knees and stiff back Hamish threw himself out of his car and ran around to the driver's side of the Subaru. He grabbed Sean by the collar through the door opening, pulling him to safety before the car plowed through the wooden fence and followed Gus over the cliff.

Hamish's limbs were trembling, and he was having trouble breathing. Sean was lying on the ground, still unconscious, his head lolling back. Pulling himself together after a few moments, Hamish checked Sean's pulse. He sighed with relief. *At least he's alive.* Then he called 911.

An ambulance's mournful wail was heard 15 minutes later. The EMT, a young man wearing a white lab coat, parked the vehicle and checked out Sean, who was starting to stir. "He should be OK, though he may have a concussion. I'll get him to the hospital where he can be fully examined. There was another victim?"

Hamish pointed over the cliff. "He's down there somewhere."

The EMT leaned over the part of the fence that remained and looked down, noticing a wrecked car twenty feet below and a body beside it. Gus was spread eagled on the rocks at the base of the cliff. "That will have to be a job for the fire department, getting his body up. By the look of him, I doubt that he'll need hospital services though. I'll try to get them here as quickly as possible to see if he's still alive." He radioed the fire department and described the situation.

An RCMP cruiser pulled up in a screech of tires, its lights flashing. Joe Washington jumped out from the passenger side. He barked at the constable who had been driving the car to cordon off the area. Hamish looked into the back seat where he could see a young woman, who waved to him. Sophie seemed in good spirits, her face flushed and her posture relaxed.

Going over to Hamish, Joe said in a reproachful voice: "So you and Sean went ahead with your plan to trap Farthing. You're lucky Sean didn't get killed, and Sophie too. She called 911 after warning you that Sean was in trouble. I picked her up on my way here. She's fine, but I sent for an ambulance to take

Farthing to the hospital. In the meantime, the constable I left there is securing the house."

"Joe, I can assure you that we did not plan this. In fact, we tried to talk Sophie out of it. But she was determined to stop this exploitation of young women. Why didn't you do your job and discover what was going on at UModel? It's not as if I didn't warn you!"

As they were talking, Sean sat up groggily, and rubbed the back of his head. Seeing Hamish and Joe beside the RCMP cruiser, he asked: "What happened?"

Washington did not respond, so Hamish spoke up: "I'll give you the details later, but Sophie is safe and sound. Jerry and Gus, on the other hand, not so much."

After the EMT had taken Sean to the hospital, Washington warned Hamish that he and Sean would need to make a full statement of this afternoon's events as soon as possible. The RCMP urgently needed to know what they had learned about Farthing's activities. "Sophie has already described the situation, but I'll also need formal testimony from her and Sean before we file charges against Farthing. Depending on what we learn, we may also decide to proceed against others associated with UModel. As for Gus, if he survives, we have enough evidence of his attempts to kill you and Sean that he's going to be put away for life."

20

Olivia

Sean didn't need to spend the night at the hospital, but had returned to his home and spent a restful night curled up in his bed with Stanfield beside him. The next morning at breakfast, Sean and Hamish did a recap of the previous day's events.

"I'm so glad you and Sophie are both all right," Hamish said. "I drove her back to Windsor while you were at the hospital. Obviously, her parents were waiting anxiously for her to get back home. She had phoned them shortly after calling me to tell them she was OK."

"Well, you sure arrived in the nick of time!" Sean said, munching on a donut and seemingly none the worse for his near-death experience. "I hate to think what would have happened if you hadn't rammed into the door of my Subaru. If you had stopped he probably would have shot you and carried out his plan to push on the accelerator while standing free as the car went over the cliff."

"It was a good thing I was waiting only a few kilometres away, so when I got Sophie's call I could reach you before Gus was able to stage the fake accident."

"As we expected," Sean continued, "there's been something very evil about UModel's operations. It's been used as a tool for people like Farthing to attract young women for sex, with the connivance of Andy Leipzig. What we don't know is whether others are doing the same thing as Farthing. And we still don't know the role played by Larry Rizzo. At least now the RCMP is involved. I just hope that they pick up Leipzig before he skips town."

Hamish nodded his head, and added, "The question is, where do we go from here? We need to let the RCMP's investigation of UModel run its course. Now that we've given them evidence of wrongdoing they're finally taking it seriously, and will lay charges against Farthing and Gus. But we're no further ahead in finding the killer of Larry Rizzo, and why someone appears to have tried to frame you for it."

"That's true, but what can we do about it? What do you suggest?"

"I think Olivia has the key to the mystery of Rizzo's murder. She must know more about all this than she lets on. What was she doing the night of his death, when she conveniently claims she was staying with her parents? We're going to need her to come clean. I know you think that she's as pure as the driven snow, but she's going to have to answer some hard questions, not just evade them as she has done."

Sean shrugged his shoulders. "And how do we go about that? We can't exactly compel her to talk, against the advice of her lawyer."

"We'll have to work on that aspect of it. Is there anyone who knows her well you could talk to?"

"Tell you what, I'll go see Danny. He hears more gossip about what's going on in this town than anyone else I can think of. I'll see what he says."

*****

It was a slow late afternoon at Danny's Bar and Grill. For some reason there were not the usuals from Morrison's Pulp and Paper Mill knocking back a beer after their shift ended at 4 pm. The rainy weather might also have discouraged some people from venturing out.

Sean sat at the bar and ordered a Moosehead. As he expected, since Danny wasn't busy he was eager to chat. "I hear you and Hamish, with the help of a young woman, caught someone with his pants down, figuratively speaking." He laughed. "And I guess it's got the RCMP to look into that UModel outfit. Glad to see you came out of it in good shape! You might have ended up like that other guy, on the rocks!"

"Yeah, I really feel sorry for him." Sean wore a smile that belied his words. "The RCMP want his testimony, but he's still in a coma."

"Well, it was either him or you. Hamish sure saved your bacon! It seems that you were about to go over the cliff."

"I'll be forever grateful to him, but I wish he hadn't wrecked my car!" Sean pretended to be pissed, then he laughed. "But we still haven't figured out why Rizzo was shot, nor who did it."

Danny scratched his chin. "You know, I probably shouldn't say this to you, but I think Olivia had picked up again with Anthony Thompson before Rizzo's murder. They were an item years ago but more recently, when her marriage was turning sour, she was also hanging out with Anthony here in town. Rizzo was usually in Halifax, so Olivia wanted company, and Anthony was close by. I've seen them have dinner together here a couple of times. Mind you, I'm just supposing they were sleeping together -- I don't know for sure."

Sean looked glum and, in order to change the subject, ordered another beer. Danny moved down the bar to serve a customer and they didn't resume the conversation. Sean left soon after.

On his way back home, he decided to stop at Olivia's house on Harrow Place. He rang the bell, waited, and was about to leave when she opened the door.

"Hi Sean! How are you doing? I hear you had a rough time with Farthing and his driver."

"Yeah, that wasn't fun. Good thing Hamish came by in the nick of time, or I would have been roadkill. Can I come in for a moment?"

"Sure. Come on through, I'll show you the renovations that have been done downstairs." The kitchen was now equipped with the most modern appliances, and an island with four bar stools on one side looked like a nice entertainment area. The living room showed evidence of recent plastering, though it was still largely absent of furniture. A sun room had been added at the back of it, with floor-to-ceiling windows and planters filled with dirt, but no vegetation yet. A pair of chairs and side tables flanked a sofa. "We could sit out here. Would you like a beer?"

Sean hesitated, then shook his head. "I just had a couple at Danny's. In fact, that's why I came. He told me that you and Anthony Thompson were an item. And maybe you still are. Is that true?"

Olivia's head jerked up, and she said angrily: "What business is that of yours?"

Sean glared at her. "You hired me to look into your husband's business after not seeing me for 30 years. Then I get called to your house, apparently by you, though you deny it later, and I discover Larry's body. That makes me the RCMP's suspect number one, so your actions are my damn business! You told me that you weren't romantically involved with Anthony, but that was a lie. For all I know, you and Anthony plotted to kill your husband, setting me up to take the fall."

Olivia's expression softened, and she bowed her head. "Fine, I guess you deserve an explanation. You're right, I was seeing Anthony. Larry had changed, he was bothered about something and didn't have much time for me. I started spending more time here in Old Town, alone, and since Anthony lives close by, we started running into each other. We've been going out together off and on since high school. But I'm not in love with Anthony, as I was with Larry, and I would never plot to kill anybody." She teared up and stared at him earnestly, as if pleading for him to believe her.

Still glaring at her, Sean shook his head. "Then explain who made that phone call to me. It sure as hell sounded like you. Do you own another cell phone? The call was made somewhere around here, at or outside the house, according to the RCMP."

"It wasn't me. I was staying at my parents' house, after my argument with Larry, and also to get away from the noise and dust from the renovations. The workmen installed the kitchen then. And I couldn't have driven out here at four in the morning because my car was in the garage getting repaired. I had to get my parents to pick me up in their car when I left Harrow Place."

"So how could I have been fooled into thinking that it was you on the phone? Even half asleep I recognized your voice. Are you suggesting I was dreaming?"

"I'll bet if the police find the phone you'll have the answer to that. I don't have a clue."

Sean looked at her sceptically. "You don't know whose phone it is then?" She shook her head. Sean went on: "OK. Then tell me about Anthony. Is he mixed up with Farthing in luring young women from UModel into sexual acts?"

Olivia turned red. "That's pretty direct!" She hesitated, then continued: "I don't know for sure, but something happened at Farthing's party that makes me suspicious. He apparently shared a glass of champagne with Jerry and your nephew's daughter Kimberly in the back room of the house. I never actually saw them though. The room was empty when I got there."

"You didn't ask him about it?"

"I haven't seen him since the party."

"So tell me another thing: was Larry in cahoots with Andy Leipzig in providing women to Jerry and Anthony?"

"I don't think so, but to be sure I hired you to look into his business activities. One thing I do know, Larry would never have procured girls for Anthony. They were mortal enemies, and have been since high school."

"Yeah, I remember. Did Larry ever admit to you that he'd trashed Anthony's car?"

Olivia looked annoyed. "I'm not going to answer that!"

"So Larry and Anthony never had anything to do with each other? They never met, even though this house is close to Anthony's?"

"Not to my knowledge. They lived in different worlds."

"But you were the link between them. Did Larry suspect you were seeing Anthony?"

Olivia, paused, thinking, and then said: "No, I don't think so." She twisted her hands, distraught.

They talked a few minutes longer, then Sean said he had to get back. On his way out, he said to Olivia: "If you ever come across that other cell phone, make sure to let Joe Washington know."

21

The RCMP's Investigations

Jerry Farthing was in police custody, accused of sexual exploitation and sexual interference of under-age females. The RCMP searched his mansion, and found hidden cameras and videos of him with young women. They were in the process of tracking them down to get their testimony. Hamish shared the names he had found in the files in Rizzo's study with Joe Washington, as well as the conversations Hamish had had with some of them. Farthing was denied bail since he was judged to be a flight risk. It was expected that other charges would follow.

Gus was still in a coma. He was guarded by a police officer stationed outside his hospital room. Based on the testimony of both Sean and Sophie, he was charged with attempted murder and aggravated assault. It was likely that he would also be charged with crimes associated with sexual exploitation.

Detective John Charles of the Halifax Regional Police's Criminal Investigation Division was instructed to search the Halifax offices of UModel. It was now two days after Sophie's visit to the Farthing house. Accompanied by a constable and bringing a search warrant, he visited the building on Connaught Avenue. The door was locked and the office was dark. The constable took out lock-picking tools and opened the door. The inner office showed evidence of a hasty departure. The filing cabinets' drawers were pulled out, and their contents had been removed. There were a few loose pages on the floor. Charles picked them up and glanced at them, but they were only utility bills. A desktop computer remained, but it was missing its hard drive.

A similar scene greeted Detective Charles at Andy Leipzig's flat. The clothes closet contained only an old pair of Nike running shoes, and a few discarded clothes. His car was not in its parking space under the building. It was evident that Leipzig had cleared out.

Charles called the phone number of the Connaught Avenue building's manager. "Do you know the name of the receptionist at the modelling agency in 310? Who signed the lease, and what was their contact information?"

The man at the other end of the phone call said he would check the files, and came back a few minutes later. "The lease was signed by Andrew Leipzig. It gives a Los Angeles address for him. I don't have the names of any of the staff. There's another interesting bit of information, though. Since Leipzig did not have a Canadian address, the lease was co-signed by a certain Anthony Thompson, of Ashcroft-by-the-Sea."

*****

Joe Washington's mail included a large envelope with a return address from a lawyer's office in Halifax. The enclosed letter read: "I have only recently learned of the death of Larry Rizzo, who was my client. He entrusted me with certain documents which he asked that I send to you in case he died in suspicious circumstances." Washington opened a second, smaller envelope that accompanied the letter. Inside were pictures of Thompson with a girl, or young woman. The photos had date stamps, and on their back was a handwritten name: Carrie Laporta.

*****

Robert Klijs went before a justice to obtain a search warrant of Anthony Thompson's residence to seize any documents related to UModel, on the grounds that UModel was a criminal enterprise and that Thompson's guarantee of their lease indicated his involvement in their illegal activities. Having received the search warrant, he immediately executed it by showing up at Thompson's townhouse in Old Town.

It was 10 pm when he rang the bell at Thompson's townhouse, pressing the button for a good five seconds. He was about to force the door when Anthony opened it. Surveying the two policemen with a disdainful air, he said: "What is this about?"

Klijs looked him in the eye and said: "I am executing a search warrant." He showed the warrant to Thompson, and walked in, forcing the latter to back up. "I would ask you not to impede us in doing our duty," he said gruffly.

Thompson was furious. "I'm going to contact my MP about this! My father knows the head of the RCMP for Nova Scotia! You're going to be out of a job soon!"

Klijs shrugged his shoulders but did not reply. He first walked around the house, looking into all the rooms. Turning to his deputy, he said: "Search the bedrooms. I'll start with the study."

Access to the study was through a door from the living room. The study contained a bookcase made of mahogany, a roll-top desk, and a grey metal file cabinet. Several framed antique maps were hung on the walls. Pointing to the desk and file cabinet, he asked Thompson: "Are these locked? If so, would you open them for me?"

"And what if I don't? I protest!"

"If you don't, we may have to force them open. We'll not be responsible for any damage."

Thompson grudgingly went to get the keys, and unlocked both. He spread his arms as if being hospitable and said with a sneer: "Help yourself!"

The top drawer of the file cabinet contained some business correspondence. Klijs leafed through these, and set aside a few letters that had the UModel letterhead or were copies of letters addressed to UModel. A lower drawer contained some files with women's names on the tabs. Leafing through them, Klijs decided that they would have to be examined more carefully so he added them to the pile of evidence to be seized.

Klijs turned his attention to the desk, which had two drawers on its right side. The upper drawer contained stationery supplies, while the lower drawer had a small camera, some electronic equipment, and a cell phone.

He put the contents of the lower drawer, as well the files he had set aside, into a box. He called to his deputy: "Did you find anything?" Getting a negative reply, he then made a list of the things he was taking. Turning to Anthony Thompson, he showed him the list: "These are the items I have taken." In the face of Thompson's silence, he said goodnight and he and his deputy left the building, taking the seized items back to his office.

*****

Hamish was in the detective agency office at The Oaks the next morning when a call came in. "Hi Hamish, this is Joe Washington. There've been some new developments in our investigation of your auto accident and the threatening letters you received. I'd like to come by and talk to you about them."

"Sure, how about this afternoon, at 2 pm? Sean should be here then also."

When Washington arrived, he refused the offer of a cup of coffee and went right to the point. "We thought that Clement Benedict was the likeliest candidate for the perpetrator of your accident and the letters quoting Bible verses, but it turns out that he has an ironclad alibi for the week before your car crash. He was having his appendix removed. The hospital staff is certain that he did not leave during that whole week. Did you drive the car in the week preceding your accident?"

Hamish thought for a moment and confirmed that he had: "I must have taken it out two or three times, without incident."

"Then Benedict can't be our man, since it seems certain your car was tampered with in the week he was in the hospital. Of course, he might have an accomplice, but we think that's unlikely. So now we're back to Singh. I'm going to have him checked out, to see if there is any recent evidence linking him to you."

"OK, good. Any developments in the UModel case?"

"Well, as you know I'm not the one directing the investigation, but we've uncovered evidence that Anthony Thompson, like Farthing, was closely involved with UModel. A search of his house uncovered correspondence with them as well as miniature cameras which we suspect were used to film young women that Thompson had tricked into disrobing. We also found a cell phone and surveillance equipment. We're trying to unlock the cell phone but Thompson refuses to give us the four-digit code."

Sean jumped in: "Maybe that's the phone that someone used to call me, asking me to go to Rizzo's house at 4 am! How is it that you were unable to locate it? Normally you can track a phone, even if it's not on."

"This one has its battery removed, so it doesn't even communicate its location to the cell tower."

"OK, then replace the battery and I'll call the number I have on my phone. We'll see if it rings."

"Give me the number. I'll talk to Klijs when I get back to my office. Oh, by the way, Hamish, we've identified the body that you found on the property of the New Dawn residence. It's that woman, Carrie Laporta, that you mentioned had disappeared after posting on the UModel website. It looks like she was raped and then strangled."

*****

Klijs objected to the suggestion when Washington made it to him. "Carroll is just trying to hijack my investigation. You're being talked into something because he's an old buddy of yours. Everyone in this case, including yourself, seems to have been part of the 1989 class of Riverview High School. I can't figure out if you're all trying to cover up for each other." He looked both angry and dispirited.

"I'm not doing him a favour, he's doing you a favour. Don't you want to solve the Rizzo case? So far, you've got nowhere."

"I've got two suspects, the wife Olivia and Sean Carroll. I just need some more evidence to pin it on one or both of them."

"Here's all you need to do: get a new battery for the phone, and I'll call the number that Sean gave to me. We'll see if it rings. Just do it."

Klijs asked a constable to find a new battery, and Washington called the number. It rang on the phone found in Thompson's desk.

Washington smiled. "So now we are making progress on the Rizzo case. You've got a third suspect, Anthony Thompson."

"Yeah, but what does the fact that Thompson had the phone tell us? Whose phone is it? And who used it the night of Rizzo's murder? We won't know unless we can unlock the phone."

"You know what? I think I have a good guess what the code might be. Try 1989. As you said, it all goes back to then."

Klijs swiped the face of the phone and at the prompt, entered 1989. Bingo! They had unlocked the phone.

Looking at the call log, they could see that a call had indeed been made from this phone to Sean's phone in the early hours of June 23.

"Let's see what else is on this phone," Washington said. The phone was linked to a Gmail account which was a seemingly random concatenation of letters. There were no email messages, either in the inbox or in sent mail. He scrolled through the other apps.

"Aha, there's a voice synthesizer installed on the phone!" Opening it, Washington clicked one of the saved files. A voice similar to Olivia's said: "Sean? This is Olivia. Can you pick me up at my house? I need to leave! Now!"

*****

Washington invited Anthony Thompson to come into the Lunenburg detachment to answer some questions. Thompson was accompanied by his family's solicitor, the distinguished Malcolm Tapper, QC. He was now in his late 60s, with a mane of white hair, a fleshy face and a paunch covered by one of his signature flowery vests. He was immediately recognizable by those Nova Scotians who were used to watching television news. He had defended a scion of a wealthy family accused of murdering his sibling, and the wife of a politician who had bought shares in a company that had subsequently been awarded a lucrative government contract, among his more famous cases.

Tapper entered the detachment building first, and then motioned for his client to follow him in, as if he had now ascertained that it was safe to do so. The lawyer strode up to the receptionist. "We're here to see Superintendent Klijs." His body language suggested that it was a gala event that they were only too glad to attend.

The receptionist invited them to sit down, but both Tapper and Thompson remained standing, and looked around as if disappointed by the lack of canapes and glasses of champagne.

After a few minutes, Klijs appeared and shepherded them to the interview room. After they were seated, Tapper started by saying, "I would like it to be on the record that my client has come of his own free will. He has nothing to hide, and is completely innocent of any real or imagined crimes."

Klijs ignored this, and said: "Mr. Thompson, I have a few questions concerning your involvement with the activities of UModel. You have the right to remain silent and to consult your attorney. Can you tell me when you started hiring, or trying to hire, models from that online agency?"

Tapper answered for him. "My client would have to consult his files to answer that question, but you are in possession of his files, so he is unable to respond." Tapper's smirk seemed to indicate that he had prepared this witticism in advance.

Turning once again to Thompson, Klijs continued: "I have a letter in front of me that indicates that last year you paid $20,000 to UModel for advertising services. What were the services that were the counterpart to that payment?"

"My client is not in possession of the necessary records, so cannot answer that question."

"Then let me turn to an item that was found in the drawer of his desk, a cell phone with a voice synthesizer app that contains a recording that purports to be the voice of Olivia Rizzo, Is that your phone?"

"My client has no comment."

"Mr. Thompson, where were you around 4 am on June 23rd of this year?"

Anthony looked down, and didn't say anything.

His lawyer said indignantly: "This has nothing to do with UModel. The interview is over!"

Klijs couldn't restrain himself from putting on a little smile. "Since you have nothing to hide, but refuse to answer the question, I am charging you, Anthony Thompson, with the murder of Larry Rizzo in the early hours of June 23rd. As of now, you are in police custody."

22

Past Lies

Sean was talking to Joe Washington on the phone: "Does this mean that I'm no longer accused of giving false information to the RCMP and a suspect for the murder of Larry Rizzo? Now that you have the cell phone, you can see that I was not lying about the phone call."

Washington hesitated, then agreed that it was likely that charges would not be filed against him. "But you're still under a warning not to interfere with our investigation."

"OK, I hear you. But I'm within my rights to help Olivia discover what Rizzo was up to. Any news about Andy Leipzig? He's got to be a key witness in your case against Farthing and Thompson for sexual exploitation, as well as being an accessory."

"No, we haven't been able to locate him. It's likely he drove across the border back to the US shortly after we apprehended

Farthing. We're asking the FBI to find him and hold him for questioning, but so far they haven't tracked him down."

Sean's next went to see Olivia at her house on Harrow Place. She opened the door, wearing a house dress, her hair dishevelled and her eyes blurry. "I can't get over Larry's death, and now Anthony's been arrested. It's all too much. I can't sleep." She wrung her hands. "Do you have any more bad things to tell me?"

She led him to the kitchen, and offered him a cup of coffee from a pot that was sitting on the countertop. "OK, fire away!" she said, holding back a sob.

"Olivia, a cell phone containing a voice-synthesized message that corresponds to the call I received around 4 am on June 23rd was found in Anthony's home office. Do you know anything about this?"

"What, are you accusing me of colluding with Anthony to kill my husband? Of course I don't know anything about this!"

"Well, I guess he could have recorded your voice without your knowing and got the synthesizer to mimic your vocal characteristics, intonation, pitch, etc. Anyway, it certainly seems that Anthony was trying to incriminate both you and me. Why would he do that to you?"

"I don't know, I don't know. I thought we were friends, but now I think that he was just using me to get back at Larry. I only learned after I married Larry that Anthony and his pals had beaten Larry up, and that was why he didn't invite me to the prom. And that it was Larry who wrecked Anthony's Thunderbird."

"So why kill Larry now? It's been thirty years, for Christ's sake!"

"I think that Larry was blackmailing Anthony. I looked over the files when Hamish returned them to me and it's clear that Larry had something on Anthony. He never discussed it with me though. I was hoping to find out by hiring you."

"And what about Anthony?"

"Whenever I mentioned my husband's name to him, he just clamped his jaws together and shut up, but I could see him seething."

Sean shook his head. "Why did you start seeing Anthony again when you knew they were mortal enemies? After all, you're the reason for their blood feud."

Olivia broke down and started to weep. "I know, I shouldn't have been so stupid. One part of me liked being fought over, like Helen of Troy. I guess I was bored with my life. Look what I've done," she sobbed.

Sean looked at her, her tears smudging her makeup, with wild hair and crows' feet radiating out from her eyes, and saw not the starlet he remembered but the middle aged woman she'd become. He wondered why he'd been entranced by her all these years.

23

Nemeses

Hamish answered the detective agency phone, and heard Sam O'Leary say: "Hamish, you know I've thought of another fellow who got out of prison who might have it in for you: Art Gibson. You never tried him, but you were the reason he went to jail in that New Dawn retirement residence scandal."

"I knew he went to jail, and lost his doctor's licence for the part he played in helping Guy Laframboise treat us retirees as guinea pigs. So he's out now?"

"Yep, he served a year of his two-year sentence, and was released on parole in April. Want me to look him up?"

Hamish thought for a moment, then said: "Sure, that's a good idea. You know, Benedict checked out OK and Singh never looked like much of a suspect, so we're out of clues."

"He's living in Halifax now. After he was defrocked he had to leave his post at the Strathcona Clinic in Ashcroft-by-the-Sea. I'll check with his parole officer and keep my eye on him."

"Thanks, Sam."

"Sure thing, Judge."

*****

Joe Washington checked out the photos that Larry Rizzo's lawyer had sent. He searched for the name Carrie Laporta on the RCMP's database and discovered that she had been reported missing the year before her body was found. The date stamped on the photos showing her with Anthony Thompson indicated that they were taken shortly after she left home.

The missing person case had been investigated without a great deal of effort by the police in her hometown on Cape Breton, and did not lead to any result. A possible link with her post on the UModel.ca's website had not been considered. Washington dispatched Constable Richard Hess to interview the neighbours of Anthony Thompson, armed with the photos.

It was blowing hard off Trahearne Bay and the occasional squall threatened to blow the cap off his head when Hess rang the doorbell of one of Thompson's neighbours. The woman in her 30s who answered the bell pulled her jacket tightly around herself but didn't invite him inside. He asked her whether she had ever seen the girl in the photograph he showed her.

The woman looked at the photo carefully, and told him she thought she recognized the girl, and had seen her coming out of Thompson's house, which was next door. "But you know, there are so many young women coming in and out of that place I can't be sure it's her. Here, let me look at it again. Just as I thought, you can see that it was taken in front of his house." She pointed to the street number that was just visible above the front porch in the photo.

The initial investigation of the body discovered by Hamish had found DNA of her rapist and presumed murderer, but their origin had never been determined. Hess arranged for that evidence to be tested against Anthony Thompson's DNA. His DNA matched that taken from under Carrie's fingernails and from her vagina. On the basis of that evidence, Thompson was charged with her rape and murder, on top of the prior charge against him that he had murdered Larry Rizzo.

*****

Art Gibson was living in a furnished apartment in Halifax's north end until he could find a permanent job. For now, he was doing the work of a paramedic accompanying EMT teams. He went out in the ambulance when serious injuries were reported.

Life in prison had been hard for someone like him who was used to the finer things in life. He had been forced to mix with people he'd never rubbed shoulders with before: drug addicts, shoplifters, car thieves, and other petty criminals. He had tried to keep to himself and bide his time in jail while hoping for parole. Thank goodness that had paid off, and now he was a free man. But he couldn't forgive Hamish Cameron for his troubles. If only he hadn't stuck his nose into the operations of New Dawn! After all, they were not hurting the residents. In fact, many of them had been doing better than expected as a result of the dietary supplements and antioxidants they were taking, retaining their mental acuity and living an active lifestyle. Then Hamish had to spoil things. Gibson particularly resented the face-to-face confrontation he had had with him and his side-kick, Sean Carroll, when they accused him of fraud and of contributing to the death of one of the residents. He wouldn't rest easy until that former judge knew what it meant to be hounded unfairly.

The letters he sent to Hamish Cameron were a good start, but he thought he had to scare Cameron by actually staging an accident in order for him to get the message. He had met someone in jail who told him he did dirty tricks on people, to make them afraid so that they fell into line and did what was demanded of them. After getting out, Gibson had paid him the $1,500 he'd asked for. The guy had gone too far though in making the accident realistic. Gibson had just asked for a scare, not an outright attempt on his life. Oh well, he didn't think they could link it to him. He would send another letter, then lie low for a while.

There was a knock at his door. He was on call, so it might be an ambulance picking him for some emergency run. Normally they called first, but maybe they couldn't this time.

He opened the door and was surprised to see a police officer outside, who introduced himself as Sam O'Leary. "Are you Gibson? Been keeping your nose clean I hope?"

Gibson just nodded, suddenly fearful.

"Well, I'll just look around, shall I? Nice place you got here."

O'Leary pushed his way into the sitting room and looked at the shabby furniture and the worn carpet. Seeing a pile of newspapers on the coffee table in front of a sofa, he leafed through them. "Aha, been cutting out some things from the *Chronicle Herald,* I see. Well well. You and I are going to take a trip downtown. I'm arresting you for attempted murder of Hamish Cameron." He put handcuffs on Gibson's wrists and herded him out the door of his apartment and down to the police cruiser.

24

The Trials

Jerry Farthing sat beside his lawyer in the Halifax courtroom, charged with sexual exploitation of Sophie Strassen and several other women. He wore a bandage that covered the left half of his face, and he was missing one of his teeth. He did not say anything to his counsel as he waited for the trial to begin, just sitting glumly and staring at the table in front of him.

The clerk called for order in the court, and Justice David Warren entered and sat at the bench. He was a small man, with thinning hair and a tired look. Turning to the packed courtroom, he said, "The Crown versus Jerry Farthing. Mr. Farthing, you are accused of sexual exploitation. How do you plead?" The assembled audience, which consisted mainly of journalists, many from out of province including some from the United States, listened attentively.

Dwight Sherman, QC, stood up and answered for his client. "My client pleads guilty, Your Honour." Sherman had impressed on Farthing the advantage of pleading guilty, given the weight of the evidence against him. There was nothing to be gained by allowing the testimony of women victims from being splashed across the front pages of leading newspapers. Several journalists rushed out to file their story in time for the evening edition of their paper.

The judge called a recess while he considered the sentence. Given the admission of guilt and the statement by Farthing that he was profoundly sorry for what he'd done, the sentence was five years in prison, not the 14 years maximum sentence allowed by the Criminal Code. After serving his sentence Farthing was to be deported back to the United States.

*****

The jury trial of Anthony Thompson before the same Justice Warren on the charge of the murder of Larry Rizzo took place a month after the sentencing of Jerry Farthing. Thompson was represented as usual by the family's lawyer, Malcolm Tapper, QC, who was wearing one of his signature floral vests. Unlike Farthing, Thompson entered a not guilty plea, with the encouragement of Tapper, who relished the publicity that a high profile trial would bring him.

The Crown counsel was an energetic woman in her forties, Mary Bullen, with a no-nonsense manner. She called Robert Klijs to the stand. Klijs presented the evidence linking Thompson to the call made to Sean Carroll the morning of June 23rd that led him to discover the body. He explained that the phone was found in his possession. He played for the jury the recording that purported to be Olivia Rizzo's voice but was actually synthesized from fragments of her speech. The Crown alleged that Thompson had rung the doorbell of the Rizzo house at 17 Harrow Place at around 4 am, and when Larry Rizzo answered the door, had shot him in the chest. The presence soon after of Sean Carroll was intended to direct suspicion onto him and away from Thompson.

When it was his turn to cross examine the witness, Tapper rose and looked over with an easy smile in the direction of the jurors, as if in no doubt that the Crown's case would not stand up. He addressed the RCMP officer. "Now Mr. Klijs, can you tell the jury whether you found any evidence linking my client to the phone that was found in his desk? Were his fingerprints on the phone?"

Klijs stuck out his chin. "The phone was found in his desk, in a locked drawer. But there were no fingerprints on it. It had been wiped clean."

"But the defendant claims that he found the phone on the ground near his house, which I remind the jury is close to the Rizzo mansion. Don't you agree that this is a perfectly reasonable explanation?"

Klijs was unwilling to grant the point, but he grudgingly said, "I guess it is possible."

"No further questions of this witness."

Crown counsel Bullen next called Joe Washington to the stand to provide a motive. Washington was clearly nervous. He was testifying both as a policeman and as a long-time acquaintance of both the victim and the accused, not to mention the victim's wife.

"Superintendent Washington, what can you tell us from your own experience about the relations between the victim and the accused?"

Washington explained that it was well known that the two men had been bitter enemies going as far back as high school. He himself had witnessed a fight between the two of them, when Thompson told Rizzo to keep away from Olivia Lopes. They had kept out of each other's paths for twenty years, but their feud had revived after Rizzo's return to Nova Scotia and his marriage to Olivia. By chance, Anthony Thompson had become involved in financing UModel, thanks to his connections to Jerry Farthing, and he was also a close neighbour of the Rizzo's, who had bought a large home near to his townhouse.

The Crown counsel then asked Washington to present to the court the photograph of Carrie Laporta coming out of Thompson's house that had been sent to him by Rizzo's lawyer after his death. The date stamp showed that the photo had been taken after she was reported missing and shortly before she was thought to have been murdered. This piece of evidence, if Anthony Thompson had in fact known of it, would have been considered a mortal threat to him.

Tapper started his cross examination by taking the witness through the theory of a feud between Rizzo and Thompson. "Superintendent Washington, do you have any evidence that the teenage rivalry between the two men has lasted to this day? Have they been seen together, arguing or fighting? Is there any correspondence between them about this alleged feud?"

Washington paused before answering. "No, but it was generally accepted that they were keeping out of each other's way so that their feud would not boil over."

Tapper smiled condescendingly. "I asked for evidence, not rumours. I have no further questions."

The judge then asked Tapper to present his defence.

He turned to the judge. "I would like to call Olivia Rizzo to the stand."

Olivia seemed nervous as she walked to the witness box. She was wearing a black dress, though it had been over a year since her husband's death. She placed her hand on the bible and gave an oath before God to tell the truth, then sat.

Tapper approached the witness box deferentially. "Mrs. Rizzo, were you aware of any ill feeling between your husband and Mr. Thompson that could have led to this tragedy? Did your husband ever mention Mr. Thompson in any context?"

Olivia shook her head. "No, his name never came up in conversation with my husband."

"Do you know of any resentment between them in recent years?"

"No, there was no evidence of that."

"No further questions, Your Honour."

The Crown counsel chose not to cross examine the witness, so the trial proceeded to concluding arguments..

The Crown argued that Rizzo clearly had evidence that the defendant had lured under-age women to have sexual relations with him. Thompson must have learned or surmised that Rizzo had that evidence. That was the reason the accused murdered him. Whether there was proof that Rizzo had actually threatened him was not central to the case, but it seemed likely that ill will between the two of them had led Rizzo to try to blackmail Thompson.

The defence argued that the prosecution's evidence was purely circumstantial. Tapper concluded his rebuttal of the Crown's case by saying: "There is no proof that Thompson fired the shot that killed Rizzo. Indeed, no weapon has been found and there is no witness to the crime. Moreover, the Crown's contention that Rizzo had material that he might use to blackmail Thompson does not prove that he actually did so. Hence, the alleged motive for the crime is hypothetical at best. There is no record of communication between them, much less evidence that Rizzo made any threats or demands on my client. As for the feud between the two of them that is alleged to have lasted thirty years, this is pure speculation on the part of the Crown." With that, he stuck his thumbs in his vest pockets, smirked at the jury, and sat down.

The jury deliberated for a day and returned a not-guilty verdict.

*****

Thompson was next tried for the rape and murder of Carrie Laporta, with Malcolm Tapper once again defending him. The Crown dwelt on the horrible crimes that had been committed, describing in grisly detail the condition of the body. At one point, a jury member was so affected by the painful testimony that the court had to be recessed for an hour to allow her to recover.

When court resumed Constable Hess presented the DNA evidence that clearly linked Anthony Thompson to the rape and murder of the dead girl. No other traces of DNA were found at the gravesite, but an examination of the outbuilding that formerly housed employees of New Dawn revealed that it had been the location where Carrie Laporta had been kept. The Crown contended that Thompson had found a way in, either with a key or as a result of picking the lock, and had imprisoned the victim there for a time, before killing her. He further presented photos taken by Larry Rizzo and provided to the RCMP by his lawyer that showed that Thompson had been seen with the girl shortly before the time she was killed.

Tapper's defence was less confident and persuasive this time. He tried to pick holes in the Crown's evidence, but his covert glances at the jury's reaction suggested to him that he had not scored many points. He exhaustively questioned the procedures used for collecting the DNA evidence and matching it to Thompson's, since that was the core of the Crown's case. Despite suggesting that there might have been a mistaken identification or a mix-up of the samples, he was unable to get any traction. In closing, he could do no better than question how an upstanding citizen like Thompson could be thought capable of such a heinous crime. He did not seem too surprised by the guilty verdict and the sentence of life imprisonment. Despite this, he loudly denounced what he called a witch trial and convinced the Thompson family to appeal. Thompson would begin his jail sentence in the meantime.

Anthony Thompson also faced civil charges. He was successfully sued by a group of women who had posted on the UModel.ca website and whom he had molested or had fraudulently lured to his apartment. Hamish had gotten back in touch with Natalie Short and put her in contact with a lawyer who specialized in sexual harassment cases. Hamish shared with the lawyer the names of other women victims, and a class action suit was brought against UModel and Anthony Thompson. The judgement in favour of each of the women in the amount of half a million dollars considerably reduced Thompson's net worth -- not that he was going to be in a position to enjoy spending his money any time soon anyway.

*****

As for Gus, whose full name was Augustin Perel, he was judged not fit to stand trial. He was likely to spend the few months that remained of his life in a hospital bed.

The RCMP's request to the FBI to help locate Leipzig for questioning on his role in exploiting young women in Canada led the FBI also to investigate his activities in the US. Andy Leipzig was eventually found by the FBI, which had connected him with exploitation of under-age women in the United States. As a result, he was accused of multiple counts of procurement during his time in LA. He was tried in California, found guilty and sentenced to ten years in prison.

UModel.ca and UModel.com websites were closed. Their assets were seized and used to compensate victims of their scam.

25

Life Goes On

Olivia Rizzo decided to put her house in Ashcroft-by-the-Sea up for sale. She would move back to Halifax, but not to Larry's luxury apartment, which she also listed for sale. Instead, she had bought a much more modest one-bedroom apartment downtown, not far from the publishing house's offices where she worked.

She came round to The Oaks to say goodbye one late fall morning, wearing an unglamorous pair of slacks and a top that might have come from Walmart. Sean poured her a cup of coffee from a freshly-brewed pot and offered her a donut. After a sip, Olivia said: "This has been a terrible year. To have my husband murdered and then to learn that someone I considered a friend of mine probably killed him has been devastating. I have to get out of Ashcroft. It just holds too many bad memories for me."

Sean sympathized with her. "To think that the events in high school would come back to haunt us 30 years later! Larry and

Anthony must have nursed a hatred for each other all of those years. They were just waiting for the right time to exact their revenge. I'm guessing that's why Larry took those pictures of Anthony with various young women. Larry got his revenge all right, but only from the grave."

Olivia wiped away a tear. "And it's all my fault! I was the prize that the two of them fought over in grade 12. If only I had never become friends with Larry, never raised the hope that I would go to the prom with him! That started the feud. And I should never have married Larry nor dated Anthony!"

"Larry must have thought that he had a trump card, the pictures of Anthony with Carrie Laporta. But there are still some mysteries. How did he know that Carrie had been murdered? Did Anthony know that Larry had evidence that would link him to her murder? Why else would Anthony kill him when he did?"

Olivia bit her lip. "Larry told me that he had come across something interesting about 'my friend Anthony,' as he put it. That's why he came down from Halifax on the evening of June 22nd. He wanted to confront Anthony. He must have called and threatened him or demanded money. Maybe he knew I'd started seeing Anthony again, I don't know. Oh God, why did I have to get entangled with those two men! I think Larry only married me to prove that he was as good as Anthony, and Anthony dated me just to get back at Larry!" She started sobbing.

Sean put his arms around her. "Don't be too hard on yourself. It could be that my going to the reunion was the trigger. Larry heard that you had asked me to investigate his activities. He may have thought that he needed to settle things once and for all with his rival and put this behind him. So he threatened

Anthony, revealing the fact that he had evidence that might send him to prison for the rest of his life. And it did, though only after Larry's death."

"I can see that now. Larry must have tried to blackmail him. That's also probably why his files contained the escort service receipts for various other men."

Sean went on, "Anthony for his part must have decided that murder was the only way out. For once, his wealth and family connections weren't going to be enough to save him. Moreover, with me now involved he had the perfect fall guy. If he could get me to go to your house then he could hope that the police would pin the murder on me. He must have picked up the Seven-Up can I gave you at the reunion and thrown it into the dumpster at Harrow Place, knowing that my fingerprints were on it. Using that synthesizer to imitate your voice was a clever way to get me on the scene, since he figured the police wouldn't believe me when I claimed to have received your call."

Olivia was sniffling, seemingly about to burst into tears once more. Sean tried to calm her down. He put his arms around her again, and hugged her to his chest while patting her gently on the back. "It will take time, but you'll get over the pain. You're young enough to start a new life. I could visit you in Halifax occasionally, if you'd like."

She hugged him back, giving him a wan smile. "Yes, I'd like that."

26

Two Years Later

After visiting Olivia a few times in Halifax, Sean belatedly admitted to himself that they had few things in common. He finally concluded that Olivia had just been using him, and he suspected that she was part of the reason that he had become a suspect for Larry Rizzo's murder. He thought that she and Anthony had been closer than she was willing to admit.

Sean saw that her interests were elsewhere, and they slowly drifted apart. A younger man was often seen with her, a budding writer who was hailed by the media as the new star of Can Lit. Sean stopped going to Halifax to visit her.

Sean returned to Marjoree Price, humbly asking for her forgiveness, which she freely gave. "Listen Sean, let's just make the best of the time that remains for us on this earth. Neither of us is a teenager anymore, we each need to look life straight in the face and decide what's most important. For my part, I think you're a kind, caring individual and we have similar things that we like to do. That's all I care about."

Hamish heartily approved of Sean's decision, which he considered was evidence of his return to sanity. "You were taken in by that woman. Nostalgia for your high school days and the enchantment of an unrequited teenage romance took over your common sense. As we get older, we tend to want to relive the past, which with the passage of time seems to us happier than it actually was. I'm glad that you're over her."

Sean changed the subject. "The good thing about this case is that we broke up a truly evil outfit that exploited young women by promising them the glamour and riches of fashion modelling. Like others before them, Farthing, Leipzig and Thompson took advantage of the naivety of youth and relied on the girls' shame to avoid being called out. Hopefully, tolerance for this sort of behaviour will soon be a thing of the past."

Hamish nodded his agreement, but fell silent. He mused about the ability of pretty women to enslave men, like Circe in Greek mythology or Helen of Troy. Instead of the face that launched a thousand ships, Olivia had broken at least three hearts and launched a vendetta that led to her husband's death and the imprisonment of her lover. That was damage enough. He also bemoaned the evil that men wreaked on others, both women and other men. Fortunately, the culprits in this case had received the punishments they deserved.

About the Author

I am a retired economist living in Niagara-on-the-Lake, Ontario, and have published extensively on various aspects of international economics and macroeconomic policy.

My hobbies include running, gardening, and sailing. I have published stories on sailing in *Chesapeake Bay* and *Sail* magazines.

More information about my detective series, *The ABC Files*, can be found on my website, **paulmassonwebsite.com.** I would welcome your feedback: you can email me using the "Contact Us" form there. To receive advance notice of new novels and a prequel of *The ABC Files* click the Newsletter sign-up page.

My detective novels can be found on Amazon and on Goodreads. If you enjoyed this book, please consider submitting a review.